SKATEWAY
TO FREEDOM

SKATEWAY TO FREEDOM

A NOVEL BY

ANN ALMA

Best wishes,
A. Alma

An imprint of
Beach Holme Publishing
Vancouver, B.C.

This book is published by Beach Holme Publishing, #226—2040 W. 12th Ave., Vancouver, BC, V6J 2G2. This is a Sandcastle Book.

We acknowledge the financial support of the Canada Council for the Arts, the Government of Canada through the Book Publishing Industry Development Program (BPIDP) and the assistance of the Province of British Columbia through the British Columbia Arts Council for our publishing activities and program.

THE CANADA COUNCIL FOR THE ARTS SINCE 1957 | LE CONSEIL DES ARTS DU CANADA DEPUIS 1957

Canada

Editor: Joy Gugeler
Typeset and Cover Design: Joy Gugeler and Jen Hamilton

Canadian Cataloguing in Publication Data

Alma, Ann
  Skateway to freedom

  "A Sandcastle Book."
  ISBN 0-88878-405-8

  I. Title.
PS8551.L565S55 1999   jC813'.54   C99-091193-0
PZ7.A444S55 1999

For Cathy Ross
who was there
when I arrived.

ONE

"Josephine, this is a family secret. If you tell anyone, I will go to jail."

Father's usually friendly blue eyes glared like ice. Josie shivered. She set the plates on the table, while Mother put a basket with six slices of bread in the middle next to the sausage, cheese and home-made jam.

"Eva, I haven't told you what happened today because this plan is between Hans and ourselves."

Pouring two cups of tea, Mother put one by Father's plate then sat down. Josie reached for her milk.

"This evening at 9:30..." Father leaned closer and ran his hand through his short, brown hair, then he lowered his voice as if the mice behind the grey walls might betray him.

"We leave this house; we take nothing." Father's eyes bored into Mother's. He glanced at Josie, then back at her mother before continuing.

"Hans will drive us to a lonely stretch of the border with Czechoslovakia. We'll cross from there to the Hungarian border and swim across the river to freedom."

Her mother gasped, then spilled her tea all over the bread.

"*Nicht heute nacht*, Karl. Not tonight," she whispered.

"We have to, Eva."

"Not so suddenly. We need to plan. What about your mother?"

"She has to stay. We leave tonight."

"Josephine, go to your room. I need to talk to your father." Her mother's voice trembled, and when she took her heavy glasses off, her eyes filled with tears.

Josie started to say "*Mutti*," but when her father waved his hand, she fled from the room. She ran down the stairs, unlocked the bicycle, wheeled it out and pedalled up the hill. By the time she reached the top, her heart beat so fast her whole body shook. Her breath screamed through her throat like the factory's staccato whistle.

She raced on to the meadow where she dropped the bike and slumped in the grass. At first only black circles swirled in front of her eyes and Josie thought she might pass out. But after a moment she was able to focus again. Below her lay the river; beyond that rows of high-rise apartments emerged like large square ghosts from the smoke of the factories' stacks. On the near side of the river a few dying trees poked up out of a swamp. This gave way to a meadow of uncut brown grass that climbed the hill.

Leave Gemeinstadt? She was born here—she had known nothing else but this area of East Germany. Her father's mother, *Oma* Grün, had always lived here. A few years ago the government had demolished her home to make room for more housing blocks. *Oma* now lived in one of the apartments built on the land where her own chicken coop once stood. This was still their place.

Picking a long-stemmed weed, Josie stroked her cheek with its softness, then chewed on the other end. Father and Mother sometimes talked about the rules and restrictions they had to live with. Father said they were like prisoners in their own country. They could not speak their minds. The Berlin Wall and the borders were closed and heavily guarded, not just to keep others out, but to keep East Germans in.

Josie was not allowed to discuss her father's views with anyone because, if the Communist party heard about his opinions, they'd take him away. Josie knew what that meant. Her parents had told her how, in 1953, the Stasi, the Secret Police, had taken Mother's parents away when they demonstrated against the government in a workers' revolt. Mother, who was only two years old at the time, was put in an orphanage. When she was older, she tried again and again to find out what had happened to her parents, but she was never able to uncover any information about them.

Father had talked about leaving East Germany before. Sometimes when Father's friend Hans came to the apartment, the two men whispered about borders and foreign money. They spent a lot of time hunched over a map. But why go now? Why today, September 28, 1989?

Josie ripped the weed into pieces and threw them away. She remembered how Anna, a girl in her class, was suddenly absent from school one day. Students whispered about her family's escape to the West. When she and her best friend Greta walked by Anna's

3

home after school, the little house stood empty, the cat mewing at the door. One day the cat disappeared too. No one ever heard from them again. It was as if a hole in the earth had swallowed them up.

Crushing the last of the seed pods between her palms, she blew them from her hands and jumped to her feet. Maybe Mother had changed her father's mind. Josie pulled her bike up out of the weeds.

"*Ach nein!* Not again." The bicycle's chain dangled loosely on the front sprocket. It happened all the time; the bike was so old. Nothing ever worked. She crouched down to fix it, and by the time she finished, her hands were black with grease.

Josie wiped her fingers on the grass and headed back into town.

At home she pushed her bike inside and chained it securely. Then she locked the door, washed her hands at the back sink of the apartment block and wiped them dry on her pants. She walked down the bare hall to her apartment.

As soon as she stepped through the doorway, Josie knew: they were leaving. Her father, his broad shoulders and chest outlined in the early evening light from the room's only window, glared at the opposite wall. Mother blew her nose, put her glasses on the table and dabbed at her eyes with a handkerchief.

Josie looked from one to the other, feeling her lips tremble. She swallowed hard to push down the lump growing in her throat. She didn't want to cry. Father would tell her she had to be strong. Seeing Mother's face made her eyes water anyway.

Her mind was a sponge, slowly absorbing the consequences of her father's decision. Everything she had known during her eleven years would be gone. Never again would she race the old bike down the hill with Greta and Walt, nor swim in the river. Even worse, in the winters she would no longer skate and twirl around the frozen pond. *Frau* Müller, the coach of the Youth Organization for Skating, said Josie showed real talent. Then she recalled her father's words, "We take nothing." Did this mean her skates would stay on the nail on the bedroom wall?

"No!" Bursting into tears, Josie ran into the apartment's only other room and flung aside the curtain that hid her clothes from view. She took down her skates. The worn leather flopped back and forth in her hands and the twine that served as laces was frayed. Still she hugged this dearest treasure to her chest. It was *Oma* who had helped her get the skates. She had arranged to trade them for some sauerkraut made from the cabbages they grew together on the balcony.

"Work hard at your skating," *Oma* reminded her constantly. Often she would meet her at the pond to yell encouraging words or applaud Josie's attempt at the jumps. At times her grandmother even borrowed a friend's skates and joined in the lessons, giggling at her own fear of falling.

"You'll go far. You're good," she told Josie. "Some day you'll skate in the State competitions. You might even win and then the State will recruit you. You will go on trips...but you must work very hard."

Frau Müller agreed. They walked arm in arm, Josie, *Oma* and Greta, along the snowy road back to the housing blocks. Sometimes Josie would daydream of a time when she would skate in front of great cheering crowds.

And what about *Oma* now? Father said she wasn't coming.

"I won't go either. I'll stay with *Oma*," Josie cried. The curtain separating her sleeping section from her parents' area moved. Mother came in, sat down on the bed and blew her nose.

"This is hard, *liebchen*, but your father, Hans, and a Czech business partner worked out all the details. They've planned it for months. *Vati* even has some foreign money. It's best..." Mother cleared her throat, "for your future—for all of us." She sighed.

Josie stroked her skates. "But, *Mutti*." Tears drowned her voice. She swallowed hard. "At school they say things will get better, after all the demonstrations are over."

"For some people, maybe." Mother sighed again. "But *Vati* doesn't think it will do us any good. There may be new openness in the Soviet Union, but here people can't even speak their own minds. You know your father lost his job with the paper because he wrote anti-Communist articles." Mother's voice trembled again.

Josie felt tears dripping off the end of her chin, but she made no effort to wipe them. She had never seen *Mutti* crying like this. It frightened her.

Josie hugged her skates tightly to her chest, the blade hurting where it pressed against her ribcage. But no matter how hard she squeezed, she could not hold back her pain.

"But at school...." She cleared her throat. "At school when Friedrich wrote a bad word on his school book he was punished with the rod and he had to write 'I'm sorry' a thousand times. So why doesn't *Vati* just take *his* punishment?"

"It's not that simple," Mother said, a faint smile slipping across her face. "I'm sorry, *liebchen*. We have to leave; it's all planned."

"No, *Mutti!*" Josie jumped up, stamped her feet on the floor, then kicked her bed. "No. I'm not leaving my friends," she yelled, throwing her skates against the wall. The loud scrape of metal blades on cement shocked her. *Mutti* would be angry.

But her mother pulled Josie down beside her, put her arms around her shoulders and said, "You'll make new friends, *liebchen*. We have to go tonight. Your father is right. This is no longer our home. We're just being used by the rich Communist bosses who have power. Everything belongs to the party: the factories, the apartment blocks, the stores...."

Josie nodded. "Yes, but..."

"Well," her mother interrupted, shaking her dark hair off her forehead and pushing her glasses back up on her nose, "the factory supervisor told us the police want to put *Vati* in jail because he is writing anti-government articles and poems. His friend Johann was imprisoned today. *Vati* thinks he will be next. They might come for him tonight." Mother's arms locked tighter.

"*Vati*...put in jail?" Josie felt her heart banging against her chest. She wanted to get out, flee, get away from all the dangers in this country. She pressed tightly against her mother.

"But Greta, and my skates, and *Oma*. We have to take *Oma!*"

"Maybe she'll join us later, after we get to Canada. When we have our own home. Sleep now, *liebchen*."

"It's too early," Josie protested.

"No, it's not. Remember, we'll be on the road all night. Sleep now, you'll not regret it."

Mother left to rest in her own bed. Josie lay down, but sleep did not come easily. Muffled sobs drifted in through the cloth divider. Josie hid her head under the pillow, but it was too hard to breathe. Besides, she needed to hear *Mutti*, even if she was crying. At least she was there—close.

After a time Josie got up. "*Oma*, you must come," she whispered to grandmother's photograph which sat on the small shelf beside her bed. She smiled at the freckled face with the soft eyes and wrinkles, the wide mouth and auburn-grey hair.

Walking to the curtain, she ran her hand down two dresses, one for summer, one for winter. This old, cold-weather thing, all patched up and too small, she wouldn't miss. Her summer dress, worn only for one season, she took off the hook. Of course it was a makeover, sewn by *Mutti* from an old dress a friend had outgrown. But the colours suited her. Slipping her clothes off, Josie put the dress on. The auburn lines were the same shade as her hair, while the green almost matched her eyes.

"We take nothing." *Vati*'s words echoed in her mind. But she had to be warm, didn't she? Leaving her dress on, Josie pulled her only pair of pants and her sweater over it.

Except for *Oma*, Greta and her skates, she wouldn't miss anything else she was leaving behind. She didn't have much: two pictures of flowers on the wall, an old rag doll she never played with anymore, her yoyo, two puzzles and some old books. She picked up the skates, hugged them, then put the winter dress on the floor and arranged her skates carefully on top of them. She leaned *Oma*'s picture against one blade.

"Good-bye," she mumbled. She picked the picture up again, kissed it and put it back down.

Stretching out on the bed, Josie looked at the arrangement for a while, then closed her eyes. In Canada perhaps they would live like the people she saw on the television when Kurt invited her to watch at his house. And maybe, just maybe, they'd even get their own TV.

Josie had heard about how the others, the people in the West, lived. Every family owned two or even three new, big, shiny cars. There were no hour-long line-ups at stores. And they had clothes—new clothes, nice clothes, so many clothes they had to build separate rooms to put them all in. Children flew to school in airplanes. They had homework machines called computers, and black boxes they carried with them on the street that played music. Instead of old bicycles they rode on boards with wheels under them.

As in a dream, Josie saw herself on a pair of brand-new, white-laced skates. She twirled around and around like a ballerina. Not on the pond. In a building where people made ice. Her feet no longer hurt where the creases bit into her skin, or where the ropes cut too tightly to hold the old leather in its place. Moving—no—flying, gliding, whirling on the glassy surface, she was like Katarina Witt, the East German who had twice won the gold medal for women's figure skating at the Olympic Games; her picture had been in every paper. Even her teacher had talked about it. Josie had paid close attention, dreaming that someday she would be like Katarina.

TWO

"It's time. Hans is waiting."

"I'm sleepy." Josie turned over in her warm nest, but her mother took her arms and slowly lifted her.

"Come on, *liebchen*, time to go."

Josie sat up on the edge of the bed, slipped her feet into her shoes, snuggled into her coat for warmth and followed her mother out through the apartment. Father met them at the front door. As he led them down the street Josie took one last look, in spite of the dim light cast by the single streetlight—the tall buildings outlined squarely against the night sky, the concrete playground where they played tag and hopscotch, the lone tree in the middle and the smokestack behind it, still filling the sky. As they walked past, she touched the trunk of the tree. "You're it," she whispered.

They ducked into a dark alleyway where Hans waited in his car, his tall frame filling the driver's seat. Though his young face smiled a welcome, the tension he felt was evident in the worry lines that creased his forehead. No one spoke.

Josie fell asleep as soon as they drove off, her head on her mother's lap.

She woke again when Mother pushed her upright and whispered, "Wake up Josephine. Wake up."
Josie rubbed her eyes, stretched and yawned. She slid out of the car and looked around. The crisp cold air jolted her awake. They were in a small clearing in the woods; the trees were dark pillars surrounding them like prison bars. Josie shivered. Hugging her arms around her waist, she edged closer to Father.

Hans kissed first her father, then her mother, on both cheeks. After he shook Josie's hand, he turned to leave, but not before she had seen tears glistening on his cheeks. He got back into his car, started the engine and drove off. Silence pressed like damp earth.

Josie moved even closer to her father's side. It was hard to breathe; her throat was blocked.

"*Komm*," Father whispered. "Follow me."

They walked one behind the other, Father in front and Mother in the back. Away from the clearing, darkness swallowed the trees. They struggled like ants over the uneven carpet of leaves and needles. Roots tripped them. Branches poked them. One whipped Josie hard in the face. She drew her breath in sharply while her hand clutched her cheek. Blood trickled down between her fingers. Without breaking the stillness, she moved on, her hand pressed against the scratch to stop the bleeding. Then, suddenly, Father stumbled into a rivulet, landing in a bush on the other bank. He muttered under his breath, and his shoes squished as he stepped onto dry ground.

Josie washed her hands and cheek. They drank the cold water before moving on, never talking, only stepping cautiously, furtively, prisoners escaping. When the trees thinned, Father stopped to study the position of the stars.

Suddenly the sound of twigs snapping just ahead broke the silence. Father froze in his tracks. Josie bumped into him. Still no one spoke. Something moved away from them, snapping and trampling branches. It must have been an animal startled by unexpected visitors. For a long minute no one moved. Josie's heart pounded; her legs shook. Then her father reached back and put an arm around her shoulders. Mother came up along his other side and they stood until their breathing returned to normal.

"We have to go on," Father said at last.

For a time their journey took them steadily uphill. Josie's throat felt like sandpaper. Finally they came to a clearing where the land levelled off. Once again they could see the sky. A few stars gleamed brightly against the pitch black, but no moon was visible.

Sitting down, they rested for a few minutes, Josie's heartbeat the only sound in her ears except for an animal calling from a distant hill. Father pulled an apple from his pocket and passed it around. Chewing it slowly, sucking the sweet moisture from the pulp, Josie leaned back against a rock to look at the stars. Father had always been interested in the night sky—he said that was one of the few good things he remembered from his time in the army when he was younger. Now he studied the far-off constellations. He walked around in the clearing, turned and looked from the sky to a piece of paper.

Are we still in East Germany? Josie wanted to ask, but she dared not break the silence. Are these mountains the Erzgebirge? Will I ever come back here? How far do we have to walk? A rush of thoughts flooded her mind: I wish *Oma* had come. My feet are sore; I think I have a blister. At least my cheek stopped bleeding. I wish I had a hat.

They continued their trek, this time going downhill, until they came to a narrow path. Although they had to continue walking behind each other in total silence, there were no more branches or roots.

At last the forest opened up to a meadow. First Josie heard the rush of water in a creek, then she saw a stream glistening silver.

Sitting down on the ground, Father motioned for everyone to take their shoes off. Josie wriggled her toes, glad to give her feet a break. They stuck their socks inside the shoes, tied the laces together and rolled up their pant legs. Hanging their shoes around their necks, Father took one of Josie's hands, while Mother held the other. They stepped into the creek.

Water pushed and stroked their legs, promising a faster, more exciting journey than the one they had just made. Josie liked the feel of it. But she was glad of her parents' hands, chaining her between them as they moved slowly, step by unsure step, across the slippery rocks. The stream was icy cold. Bits of spray misted her face.

Suddenly, Father teetered, almost losing balance, jerking Josie's arm. She moaned inwardly as he gripped her hand tighter to steady himself. He regained his footing and they made their way carefully to the bank.

After rubbing their numb legs and feet dry with handfuls of grass, they struggled to put their tired, damp feet back into their socks and shoes. Father cupped his hands around Josie's ears to block out the noise of the rushing water and said, "Not much farther now."

Josie sighed with relief. She didn't think she could walk anymore, but somehow she stumbled on along the bank of the creek as her father led them onto a wider trail.

Just up ahead a dark figure emerged from the bushes. Josie's heart jumped. She turned, ready to run, but Mother put out an arm to stop her. Father walked up to the stranger. They embraced. Mother took Josie's hand and pulled her closer. Only then did Josie notice the outline of a small car, parked in a tiny clearing at the edge of the trail. They all piled into it silently. The stranger started the motor and, without turning on the headlights, drove them away. The car swung in and out of ruts on the rough road, bouncing them from side to side.

"Ouch," Josie mumbled as she hit her head, then her elbow. She clutched the seat in front of her. But soon they left the trail and turned sharply onto a paved country road. Now the driver turned the car's lights on.

Father turned from the front seat and smiled. "Eva, Josephine, this is my friend Jan. He'll drive us all the way through Czechoslovakia to the border with Hungary." Josie noticed that Father put his hand on Jan's shoulder for a moment.

"I'll take you home for a rest and something to eat," Jan said. "I live in Prague. My wife is waiting to greet you there."

Josie couldn't see Jan's face, but his voice sounded kind. And what he said was even better—a bed and food! Unable to keep her eyes open any longer, she sank into a haze of sleep, just as the sun outlined the trees in morning gold.

*

Josie woke in a bed, although she couldn't remember coming into the house. Her stomach rumbled. Slipping out from under the blanket that covered her, she noticed she was still wearing her summer dress under her pants and sweater.

Voices came from behind the door. Josie quietly turned the handle and peeked into the next room, where she saw Mother, Father, Jan and another woman sitting around the kitchen table.

"Good afternoon, sleepyhead," Father said.

Mother laughed. "Judging by your hair you had a fight with the pillow. Here." She took a comb from her pocket and gave it to Josie.

Jan introduced her to his wife, a short, heavy-set woman called Nadia. She pushed bread, butter and sausages across the table, saying, "We'll have our hot meal quite soon, but here's something to nibble on until then."

Nadia had a funny accent, just like Jan, and when they talked to each other Josie couldn't understand them at all.

Josie reached for a piece of bread. "What time is it?" she asked.

"After two o'clock."

No wonder she felt rested: she'd slept all day. "Where are we now?"

"In Prague," Jan said. "I just took your mother sightseeing. You still slept so soundly, we didn't want to wake you."

"Is Prague close to the Berlin Wall?"

"No." Father laughed. "We're not going that way. We'd get shot for sure at the wall. We're going through Czechoslovakia and Hungary to Austria. It's a long way but I think it's a safer route."

"Why?"

"It's easier to cross to the West from Hungary than from East Germany."

"When will we be in Hungary?"

"Tomorrow morning," Father said. "If all goes as planned." Josie thought she heard tension in his voice, but when she glanced up, Father was smiling.

Standing up to take her plate to the sink, Josie winced as she felt the blister on her heel. Jan took the dish from her.

"I'll get a tub of hot salt water for you," Nadia said.

While Josie soaked her feet, the adults looked at a map and discussed the upcoming drive and where Jan planned to buy gas from his friends.

"Dry your feet now." Nadia handed Josie a towel.

"What is happening in East Germany, Karl?"

"Things are coming to a boiling point," Father said. "I'm afraid of what the East German government will do to the people who dare to speak out for their freedom. So many people are leaving. Of course, it's easy to go to other Eastern Bloc countries. I've heard that trainloads of people go to Hungary. They get travel permits, then they just disappear."

"They go to the West German embassy," Jan said. "They crawl over the fence onto the embassy lawn and automatically become West Germans. I read it in a newspaper."

"Do you want to do that too?" Nadia asked. "It might be less dangerous."

"No," Father said. "We'll stick with our plan. I chose a tougher way to get out, but it's better for our future. West Germany already has too many refugees. We'll go to my cousin's place in Canada."

Less dangerous? Josie stopped tying her shoe. What were Father's plans? "What will happen to us?" she asked, looking from one adult to the next.

"Nothing, *liebchen*. Of course there is always the unexpected. There are many changes; countries opening borders and others closing them. We can't be sure where the border patrols are. They seem to be in different places every day. That's why we have to go at night, quietly." He patted Josie's shoulder.

"But *Vati*, why would it be dangerous?" Josie didn't feel at all reassured.

"Oh, let's not worry," Father said. "We'll be fine. Help Nadia."

Josie set the table. The hot meal smelled delicious. Nadia served dumpling soup, roast goose (the country's specialty) with sauerkraut and potato dumplings. For dessert, Jan ladled out hot custard pudding, but Josie only ate a few spoonfuls: she'd feasted too much on the goose.

After Jan packed some leftover meat and bread slices into a bundle to eat on the road, they went out to the car.

"With God's will...." Nadia cried openly when she kissed first Jan, then Mother, Josie and finally Father. "Be careful," she sobbed, while shutting the door on Father's side. Josie watched out the back window as Nadia waved and dabbed her eyes with her apron. They turned a corner.

Josie looked at the street. Narrow, closed in and crowded, buildings pushed each other for space.

"I know a park on a hill that is a great lookout," Jan said. "We'll just stop there."

Reaching an area higher up, they got out. Jan pointed.

"That's New Town, where we walked this afternoon, Eva. And on those hills, look, that's Prague Castle."

Josie gazed at the city stretched out like a jigsaw puzzle of roofs, church spires and parks. A river meandered through like a slippery slug's silvery trail.

"We'd better go," Father said. "We have a long journey ahead of us."

"You know, Karl," Mother took Father's hand as she leaned towards the sights, "I always wanted to explore this beautiful city. Now I'll never see more of it." But she didn't protest when Father gently led her to the car.

They drove through streets crowded with shops. Everything was bigger, closer, busier than Josie was used to. And, though from the window displays the shops seemed no different than those of Gemeinstadt, the signs above them made no sense to her at all.

Prague was much bigger than any city Josie had ever seen. Snuggling into the corner of her seat more comfortably, she began to feel the excitement of the adventure.

An hour later, as it started to get dark, they reached the countryside. There, zooming along the road, with trees, farms and hills flashing by, they could almost be in East Germany: everything looked so similar.

Josie wondered about her friend. Had Greta missed her? She had probably waited at the corner until she was almost late for school. Surely she'd checked at the apartment by now and found it locked.

"Can I write a letter to Greta?"

"What was that, *liebchen*?" Mother's voice sounded sad and tired.

"Can I write Greta?"

"We'll talk about that later, when we get settled. We've only been gone for a day."

Was that all? One day? It seemed like they'd been traveling for a week. Just this afternoon, a few hours ago, Greta might have heard students whispering about her disappearance, the way they had about Anna's. Did Greta feel the earth had swallowed Josie up too?

"I've gone, but I'm still here with you," she thought. Then, out loud, she asked, "When will we have a home again *Mutti*?"

"I don't know. Soon, I hope." Why did Mother sound so distant? Why was her voice breaking? Josie glanced over in the dark, but her mother turned to the window.

She had no home, no friends, no family other than Mother and Father, no toys or books, not even her skates. *Oma* was so far away, Josie could never drop in for cookies and tea again, or help dust the figurines her grandmother had collected over the years. They'd never walk again arm in arm from the pond, laughing and talking about skating.

Resting her head on the window ledge, Josie closed her eyes, although she wasn't really sleepy. Mother stroked Josie's hair. Shifting, she put her head on her mother's lap.

"*Mutti*, I want to go home."

"So do I, *liebchen*, so do I."

Night fell. The car grumbled on along the bumpy road, now behind a shaft of yellow light that pierced the darkness like cats' eyes. Except for rattling tools, somewhere under a seat, all was silent inside the vehicle.

THREE

Josie woke with a start. It was pitch black. Something moved beside her. It touched her sleeve. She froze with fear.

"*Liebchen.*"

Mother's voice. Of course, they were in Jan's car.

"Why is it dark? Where are we?"

"Shhh!" Mother whispered. "We're at the river between Czechoslovakia and Hungary. We don't want to be seen or heard. *Komm.*" She pulled Josie's sleeve.

They got out of the car and stood in a tight group in the darkness. Jan quickly hugged and kissed each of them in turn, then climbed back into the car and drove away, lights out. The three fugitives did not move as the sound of the engine faded away.

Taking Josie's and her mother's hand, Father led them away from the road and through undergrowth until they came to the banks of a wide river. Water lapped at their feet.

Father pulled them into a tight huddle. "Now we must swim to the other side," he whispered.

"But, *Vati*..." Josie tried to protest. The river was too wide! The current too swift! Father closed his hand quickly over her mouth.

"Don't worry, *liebchen*. Be brave. I know you can do it. The darkness makes it look farther than it is. No matter what happens, keep going. If anyone shouts at us, try to swim under water. At the far side you'll see shrubs. Crawl into them and hide. Wait there for me."

Father hugged Josie and Mother again and said, "I'll go first. Josie, you're in the middle. Eva, you come last. Try to stay close." He slid noiselessly into the water.

Her mother, who had taken her glasses off, looked like a stranger in the dark: tight fists clamped over her mouth, eyes magnified in terror. Josie started to say "*Mutti*," but was pulled into an airtight clasp, then pushed firmly out to the river.

Shaking uncontrollably, Josie slid forward, her arms spread, tears mingling with the water. The cold took her breath away. Her heart jumped. The weight of her waterlogged clothes pulled her down. She fought with her arms, thrashing the water around her. Fear gripped her, tightening the muscles in her chest so that she could not breathe. In the darkness all she could see was the terror in her mother's face.

As she struggled to stay afloat, Josie suddenly felt a hand on her stomach. Father was next to her. "Be strong," he said. "You can do this."

"Too heavy," Josie managed to whisper.

Father quickly undid the buttons of her coat and helped her out of it. It floated away into the blackness: her only coat, given to her by Mother's cousin.

"I love you," Father mouthed, before pointing to the far side. Taking a deep breath, Josie put her face in the water and swam her first two strokes. Yes, she could move. But her clothes made it difficult to swim smoothly. Her shoes were so heavy. She stopped swimming and looked for Father. Darkness closed off her world. She was alone.

If her coat could be cast off she could get rid of her shoes too. With one foot she pushed the other heel out, then shook it free. She'd hated these shoes from the beginning. The hard, brown leather had squeaked and they hurt, especially now, on her bandaged blister.

With those two anchors removed, it was easier to stay horizontal. Filling her lungs, Josie put her head down and swam as far as she could. When she raised her head for air, she could make out one other body in the water ahead of her. She breathed in again, ducked and swam several strokes. It was almost like skating, stroke, stroke down the ice. Josie pretended that *Oma* was watching her. She moved on: her head up above water, then under again.

The opposite shore seemed no closer. Was she actually moving? In that instant a searchlight flashed across the water's surface. Two shots rang out. Ducking quickly, Josie swallowed dirty water. Her throat burned with the need to cough. Her chest heaved. She tried to hold herself still. With her lungs on fire from the long wait, she came up.

Lights crisscrossed, stabs of light turning the river into a black and white game board. Josie spluttered. She inhaled. She dove down again. Came up for air again. Her wild breathing made her cough. A shot cracked; water splashed nearby. She dove deep.

All thought of the cold, the heavy clothes, the tug of the river disappeared. Now she swam as hard as she could. With every stroke she pulled herself toward her goal. When she came up for air, she glanced at the opposite bank. She dove down again, pulling herself through the water as deep as she dared. Up again and down.

Her outstretched fingertips finally bumped against the shoreline. Pulling herself up out of the water, Josie crawled onto the land. Her teeth chattered; her lower jaw shook. Gasping, she flopped down and lay still.

A beam of light crossed her path. Motionless, not breathing, she waited, her face pushed into the soil. Darkness again. With clothes clinging to her body like wet plaster, she slithered on. Dirt covered her hands and face. A heavy earthen smell filled her nostrils.

She reached the cover of the bushes along the bank. Josie crawled into the shrubs and looked around. There was no sign of life. Was it possible that Mother and Father had landed in a different area; that they didn't make it; that the shots had hit them; that they would never come for her; that morning would find her cold, lost and completely alone in a strange country.

*

Josie rolled over on the hard ground and looked around. It was dawn. At first she did not know where she was. She was damp and stiff and confused. Only the sound of birds singing reassured her. Then her father's voice came from a short way off.

"Josie." A soggy, crouching figure beckoned.

"*Vati!*"

Crawling from the bush, she ran toward her father and the forest. And there, behind a big shrub, mud-covered, stood Mother, smiling and crying all at once, her face no longer a stranger's.

"*Mutti!*" They hugged each other before sitting down to catch their breath.

"Where are we, *Vati?*" Josie's teeth chattered.

"I'm not sure. Somewhere in Hungary, if Jan and I calculated correctly."

"Where do we go from here?" Mother was okay again, Josie saw with relief. She polished her glasses and put them back on her nose.

"We find the highway to Austria."

Josie looked at the water, now barely visible through the trees, and thought of the life that lay beyond it: her home, her relatives, her friends, the freedom she had known when she was skating. It felt as if she had been washed away from all that now, like a ship swept from its moorings.

Turning their backs to the river, they started off on a path through the woods. Her parents still had their shoes, but Josie found it difficult to walk on the forest carpet in socks.

"I should have carried your shoes," was all Father said, when Josie told him how she'd kicked them off. If this had happened at home, her parents would have punished her for being so wasteful, but now they were just relieved to be together.

Father set off at a brisk pace, while Mother and Josie followed more slowly. She had to watch the ground to avoid hurting her feet. Watching her father disappear down the trail made Josie uneasy, but it wasn't long before they caught up with him. He stood beside a creek that ran along the edge of a pasture. He had washed his face and hands, rinsed some of the dirt from his clothes and smoothed down his hair.

"You wait here. I'll check out that farm over there," he said, walking off in the direction of a small cluster of buildings. Josie heard a dog barking, but saw Father walking on to greet the brown pup.

Shivering from the cold, Josie and her mother kneeled by the stream to wash off the worst of the dirt. If the mud stayed on her face any longer her skin would crack, Josie thought.

Soon Father and another man called and waved from the farm while the dog ran up, tail wagging.

"*Hallo*, Eva, Josephine, *komm hierhin*, everything is fine," Father called.

Going as fast as they could on their shaking legs, Josie and her mother crossed the pasture.

"*Hogy van?*" the farmer said, shaking hands. Josie didn't understand him, so she mumbled a greeting and followed everyone into the kitchen. There a tall woman had started a fire in the wood stove while two boys, about Josie's age, watched the pots on the burner.

"Myrna," the man said, pointing to the woman, who looked over her shoulder with a bright-eyed, smile. "Laszlo," he slapped a work-worn hand on his chest. Father introduced his family. Then Laszlo took them to a bedroom where they changed out of their wet clothes and into borrowed pants and sweaters.

"Do you know these people, Karl?" Mother asked.

"No, they're just being kind to us. I'm sure they have had others fugitives come through here."

Everyone sat around the stove for breakfast. The porridge trailed warmth all the way to her stomach and she finally stopped shivering while she listened to the adults, who, with the help of hand motions, pictures and a map, tried to have a conversation in German, Hungarian and Russian. It was strange, she thought, to be in this place where she and her parents knew nobody, but where they were welcomed. They were all part of the Eastern Bloc and had had to learn Russian as a second language. But were they free? Father seemed to think so.

"*Mutti,*" she whispered, "is there a wall around Hungary?"

"No, only around Berlin."

"Why?"

"Because so many East Berliners fled to West Berlin that the Communists had to do something to stop them. Everywhere else they have guarded border crossings with barbed wire. But here they don't. We can get out."

Mother turned back to the adult conversation while Josie wondered what the other side of the border looked like.

At last her parents understood the directions to the major highway that led to Austria.

"I think it's just twenty minutes up the road," Father said.

Myrna and Josie washed the clothes in the sink and hung them to dry on the rack above the wood stove. They wrapped Josie's summer dress in a sheet of newspaper, along with some bread and cheese for lunch. Father, Mother and Laszlo studied the map. The boys stayed in the background and whispered to each other. They found shoes and an old jacket. Josie felt shy when she accepted them. They didn't talk; just grinned and looked away.

Back into their own dry clothes, they thanked the family and said goodbye. Laszlo shook each hand in turn in his firm grip, while Myrna clasped their hands and smiled warmly. The boys stayed back. She didn't even know their names, Josie realized. In town Father took strange-looking money from a plastic bag to buy tickets. An hour and a half later they were on the bus to Austria. At the last stop before the border they got off.

"Oh, can't we go all the way on this bus?" Josie felt tired and disappointed. Were they ever going to get there?

"We have to cross the border on our own," Father said.

"We don't have to swim a river again, do we?" Josie clasped her father's arm. Her breath caught in her throat.

"No, we just walk across on the road. I'll tell the border guards that we're refugees. In Hungary they understand these things."

But if Father thought it was going to be easy, he was soon proven wrong. They approached the border crossing together, Josie between her father and mother. Father instructed them to smile, but Josie knew that her face betrayed her fear. Unfortunately the uniformed guards didn't speak much German, and they became impatient when Father repeated slowly, "We will just cross; we do not want trouble."

One of the guards seemed friendly, but another looked at them as if they were criminals. He sneered and his voice kept getting louder.

Father stayed calm. But when he took Josie's hand and tried to walk down the road, the mean guard shoved them back. Immediately two others with guns barred their way. Josie pressed close against Father, who let go of her hand and put his arm around her shoulder.

"*Komm*," one of the men said. He led everyone to an office in a small building beside the road, then pushed Josie and Mother toward a wooden bench and made them sit down. Two men took Father into another room. The door closed behind them.

"Will *Vati* be okay?" Josie whispered. If only they had left the door open and one of the men with the guns hadn't gone in too.

"He has a good plan. It'll work," Mother said. She took her glasses off, then clasped her hands tightly together, the knuckles turning white from pressure. Loud voices came through the door. Mother's face went white too.

Josie felt a queasiness in her stomach that got worse and worse until she thought she might throw up. Would they hurt Father? Or shoot him? Or take him away the way they had taken Mother's parents? Trying to block the sound of the shot she expected, Josie pushed her hands over her ears. She couldn't hold back the tears. Bending her head down to her knees, she closed her eyes. Feeling Mother's arm slide around her, she pressed closer.

Suddenly Mother pushed her upright. Josie looked and there was Father, walking out of the office, a slight smile on his face.

"Let's go," he said.

"*Vati.*" Josie ran to him and held his sleeve as they walked out. She couldn't stop shaking or crying even though they were motioned through and walked down the road. There was still another barrier a little further along the road.

"How did you convince them?" Mother asked.

"I gave them money."

At the Austrian checkpoint the border guards spoke German. Josie looked up in surprise. Father again explained their situation, holding out money. But the guard smiled broadly, refusing the bribe and welcoming them to the West.

"Don't worry, you are safe here," he said to Josie.

Her legs felt less wobbly as she waited while her parents filled out several forms. They got instructions on how to get to the refugee center in Vienna.

"Josie, we did it. We're free." Father gathered them into his arms. "Everything's fine now, *liebchen.* We did it."

They sat on a bench beside the highway to wait for the bus. No one said anything. Josie watched her parents; they were smiling and holding hands. She slid closer. Father put his arm around her shoulder and suddenly burst into, "*Freunde, das Leben ist lebenswert.*"

Mother laughed loudly. "You and your opera."

They started humming a tune Josie had often heard them play on the old record player; Beethoven. This side of the border looked the same as the eastern side, just a road and a few buildings, but it felt very different, lighter, happier. Josie joined in the humming, holding hands, all three swaying slightly from side to side.

The bus came. Father bought tickets. They found three seats together and watched the border to the East disappear.

FOUR

The next few days were a blur. Josie felt sick on the bus to Vienna and when they had their medical examinations at the refugee center a doctor found spots on her body and told her parents she had the measles. He ordered her family to stay in a separate hotel room instead of in the large hall with all the other refugees. Father said that this gave them privacy, and time to contact his cousin Fritz and get all the travel papers in order.

Three times a day Mother or Father went to the refugee center to collect a meal. They brought it to the room in small containers. The Red Cross even gave them each tooth brushes, soap, a towel, one set of extra underwear and medicine.

Josie glanced around the room from the cot she had now been on for...how many days? Four, maybe five? She wasn't sure. The ceiling light, a bare bulb, was off. The thin, blue-and-white-flowered curtains were drawn, but even so, her eyes hurt as if the sun shone right into them. Her skin prickled all over.

From her cot she could see her parents' double bed, a rickety table with a chair and in the far corner of the room her mother reading a newspaper by the light of a lamp partially covered with a towel.

Mother held the paper very close to her face, as she always did, because of her poor sight. When she was a child, on the day the Stasi took her parents away, one of the policemen had spilled something, the doctors weren't sure what, on Mother's face. Her eyes had been affected ever since: she was blind for the first few years. After that, at the orphanage, she got some of her sight back and finally started school at the age of nine.

Josie squinted her eyes. What if *she* couldn't see properly after the measels?

"*Mutti*, will my eyes be bad forever?"

"No, *liebchen*." Mother put the paper down and walked over. "You'll be fine in a few days."

"Where's *Vati*?"

"He went for a walk. How are you feeling?"

"Fine. A bit hungry." It hurt to talk.

"*Sehr gut*. It looks like you're getting better. Let me take the cloths off your hands."

Mother unwound the cotton strips, and Josie stretched and bent her fingers. Then she started scratching a spot on her cheek.

"No, no, don't scratch. That only makes it worse. Here, drink some of this broth."

Josie took a few sips, then put the cup down and automatically scratched her cheek again.

"Don't use your nails." Mother wrapped clean cotton strips around Josie's hands. Then she bathed Josie's face and upper body.

"Our travel papers are ready. We can leave when the doctor says you're better."

"Did Father find his cousin Fritz?"

"Yes. Fritz was separated from the rest of your father's family when the Berlin Wall was built. The Red Cross found Fritz's adopted parents' phone number. They're still in West Berlin, although Fritz lives in Calgary, in Canada."

Calgary. She'd heard that name before. But where? Josie tried to concentrate, although all she wanted to do was scratch. Calgary...something about skating...Katarina Witt won her gold medal at the Olympic Games in Calgary.

"Mutti, when we go there, can I buy skates?"

Mother smiled and stroked Josie's hair. "You and your skating. Just get yourself better, don't scratch, sleep a lot, and I'll do what I can to find you skates." Mother picked the paper up again and sat down.

Josie closed her eyes. Tired and dreamy, her mind floated to Canada.

When she woke again, Father sat by the lamp, reading the paper. He looked up and smiled. "You're looking a bit better."

"I feel better. Where's Mother?"

"Helping at the refugee center again. Do you feel well enough to start English lessons?"

"English lessons?" Josie looked at her father in surprise. She had expected her parents to ask her to read and do math. After all, she'd missed more than a week of school already. But why English lessons?

"In Canada they speak English. I thought you knew that," Father said.

How could she know? They studied Canada and the United States in school. But she wasn't good at memorizing things and she remembered very little. It was big and had long, cold winters, like in the USSR.

"You mean...." Josie looked at her father with the sudden shock of realization. "You mean they don't speak German?"

"No, they speak English. French too, I think. But we'll learn English."

"*Vati*, how will I make friends? How can I go to school if they don't speak German?"

"That's why we're studying English." Father tapped a tape recorder and books. "A man from the Red Cross lent these to me. We'll start when Mother gets back from the refugee center."

※

The next week, while Josie struggled to keep her hands from scratching the last of her red spots, they spent most of their time at the table, repeating strange sounds from a tape and reading words from a book. Father had learned English before, at the newspaper. Besides, he was good at languages. But Josie and Mother found the lessons difficult.

"There just isn't room for new words in my mind," Mother said one day. "My head is so full, it might burst." A tear slipped down her cheek.

"Just try a little more, Eva. These sounds will start to make sense soon."

Josie had a hard time too. She learned how to greet people, and she knew the English names for some of the objects in the room. But often Father sounded impatient when he asked her something and Josie didn't understand him. Besides, he enjoyed words, so this was exciting for him. Mother preferred to help out at the refugee center, she liked listening to others, while Josie just wanted to go home.

Instead, they worked at English all day long. Before she was allowed to use the sink Josie practiced: "I brush my teeth, you brush your teeth, he brush his teeth...."

"No, Josie, he brushes his teeth."

"*Ach ja*, he brushes his teeth, she brushes her teeth, we brushes our teeth, no, we brush our teeth, you brush your teeth, they brush their teeth."

Then came Mother's turn. "I wash my face, you wash your face...."

Most days her parents also went to the center for the latest news on East Germany. Since their arrival in Vienna, first rumours, then actual articles in the newspapers, told of changes in their old country. So many left on trains to West Germany that the police could no longer stop them. Josie saw a photograph of what they had started calling "freedom trains" loaded with cheering, waving people. In all the bigger cities, thousands upon thousands of people demonstrated against the country's leaders while the police, after years of breaking up large gatherings, stood silently and watched the crowds flood every street and city square. Sometimes they even joined the masses.

Then one day Father raced into the room, jumping, shouting and waving a newspaper.

"He's been replaced," he yelled, hugging first Mother and then Josie. "Honecker's been kicked out of the government."

Mother and Father danced around the room, laughing. Josie didn't really feel excited. Honecker was just the party leader. Giving her itchy shoulder a secret rub against the doorpost, she stared at one parent, then the other.

"Josie, things are finally happening," Father said, scooping her up and almost tossing her into the air. "People demanded freedom. Now they might get it."

"Karl," Mother grabbed Father's shoulders, "let's go to West Germany. We can wait there until things have settled. Then we can go back home where we can speak German. Maybe I can find my parents."

"No, Eva, we can't take that chance." Father hugged Mother. "Your parents are gone. After thirty-six years it's too late to look for them. We've tried before. I'm sorry, *liebling*." Father kissed Mother. "We have to forget the past. We'll be happy in Canada"

Over the next few days, as reports about people's protests continued on the news, Mother tried to persuade Father that they should stay closer to home, instead of going to the other side of the world. But Father insisted it was too risky. Now that they had come this far, they would continue.

Josie wished Mother could persuade him. She didn't want to go to a country where no one spoke German.

Mother stopped trying to speak English. She ate little. Then one morning she stayed in bed, saying she was sick. Sneezing and coughing, she began to complain about a pain in her ears.

The next day Mother's eyes and nose ran and, although she got up, she coughed constantly. With medication from the Red Cross, her head cleared a bit, but she continued to have little appetite.

Father came back with other news. "Josie, your checkup is tomorrow. If the doctor clears you, we fly to Canada on Tuesday, October 24."

Tuesday. Only a few days from now.

"Karl, I want to live in Germany," Mother mumbled, her nose and mouth covered with a handkerchief, her eyes overflowing. "It's not too late. Canada is too far away."

"Be strong, Eva. Canada is a good country. Everybody says so. They say it's a land of opportunities for refugees."

That might be true, Josie thought, but today she felt like Mother. What she wanted to do most of all was to race the old, rusty bike down the hill with Greta.

"Will we ever go back home, *Vati*?"

"We have no home. We're refugees. That means we are homeless, countryless. But Canada will be our new home soon enough."

✳

They started their trip to the Vienna airport on Tuesday afternoon. Because they travelled on stand-by to London, they had to wait for five hours before seats became available.

The parade of rushing people, short and tall, young and old, light and dark, fascinated Josie. They all walked and talked differently, and in her mind she imitated some of the more interesting ones. But after a while this game became boring. Mother wouldn't let her walk around by herself, so she stayed in the chair and waited and waited.

When they finally left Vienna, Josie watched from the plane window. Below her the buildings got smaller. It was dark out. The lights from the buildings and the moving cars created a miniature world.

At first the flight was exciting, but after a few hours Mother began to cry and Father just stared straight ahead.

There was a funny feeling in her ears, as if they were plugged and needed to pop. She sat quietly, her hands on her lap. Bored and tired, she yawned, which made her ears feel better. If only *Oma* were here.

In London they waited for another three hours before they got onto a plane to cross the Atlantic Ocean. By this time it was the middle of the night, so Josie slept for most of the flight. In the morning she looked out the window. She wished she could get out, stretch or lie down on the clouds below her. They looked soft, like *Oma*'s feather tick.

They landed in Montreal when the city was still asleep, even though it felt like daytime to Josie. Father told her it was because they were on the other side of the world now, where it was nighttime. In East Germany it was already the morning of the next day.

After hours of long line-ups and meetings with officials, at last they were allowed to leave the airport and continue their journey. The Red Cross had helped Father buy plane tickets to Montreal, because they were cheaper than a flight to Calgary. They now had to take a local bus from the airport to the bus depot.

"I hope we have enough money to buy tickets to Calgary," Father grumbled.

Mother didn't say anything. Josie just walked along beside them, too mixed up and tired to notice the city.

They did have enough money. Then Father spent the last of the funny-looking coins on a loaf of bread, a bottle of drinking water and six apples.

For the next two days, while they raced along the Canadian highway, Father gave each of them a third of an apple and two slices of bread three times a day. The bread was already cut into thin slices, something Josie had never seen before. Canadian bread smelled different and she could fold a whole slice into one mouthful; it chewed into nothing but a tiny lump of tasteless dough.

Josie stood up and wriggled her stiff body. "*Vati*, when will we be there? We've been on the bus for two days now."

"Soon, I think."

"I'm hungry."

"Get used to Canadian meal times, Josephine. We eat when everyone else does."

Josie didn't understand why her father spoke to her in such a harsh voice. Was he angry at her? Perhaps he too was frightened. Josie put her hands on her empty stomach and pressed down. There was no food left, so they had to wait until they got to Uncle Fritz's before they could eat again.

Stepping her feet up and down, Josie pretended she was a hungry soldier on a march. Then she flopped back into her seat.

Yawning, she stretched her arms above her head. For three days and nights they hadn't slept in a bed. Josie's body felt like a rolled-up sleeping bag straining to spread out on a flat surface. If she could only run around the bus a few times, like she'd done before. Her body twitched so she swung her legs back and forth for a while. And even though the bus roared along smoothly, not like in East Germany, where the roads were narrow, winding and uneven, she wished they could go faster.

Mother was right—Canada was far from home.

"Are you okay, *Mutti*?"

Mother coughed and said, "I'm tired of this bus ride too, *liebchen*, but we'll be there soon and then we'll all feel better."

Stretching, Josie stood up again between her seat and the one in front of it. Looking over the chairs in front of her and out the front windshield, Josie noticed a city up ahead. Canadians left so many lights on at night, the sky around a town or city glowed like a giant yellow ball in the darkness.

The man in the chair ahead turned and said something. Sitting down quickly, Josie realized she'd understood one word. Calgary!

"*Mutti, Vati*, this is Calgary," she whispered. "Now we can go to our new home." She felt a flutter of excitement in her stomach.

Mother gave a weak smile, but said nothing. Father looked out the window, then began talking in English to the man in front of him.

Reaching for their paper bag in the overhead rack, Father stood up and said, "Yes, we're here."

FIVE

The bus came to a stop at the Calgary terminal. Eager to be the first one out, Josie jumped up, but her mother still sat in the seat next to hers, blocking the exit.

"*Komm*, Eva." Reaching, Father took Mother's hand. "We'll soon be there and then you can sleep and get rid of that awful cold."

Mother struggled out of her seat. Josie watched her mother shuffling to the front of the bus like an old lady.

This was it; they were home! They needed to find Uncle Fritz, and he would take them to their house.

While Josie jumped off the bus a stranger in a red jacket, jeans and a funny red cap with a flame on it hurried towards them.

"Karl. *Doch!* Is that really you?"

"Fritz!"

He spoke German? Josie watched, a smile on her face, as the man hugged Father. They kissed each other on the cheeks.

"Oh Fritz, *endlich*, finally..." Father's voice broke.

Clearing his throat, he pulled Mother closer. "This is my wife, Eva."

Fritz hugged Mother too, then turned.

"And you must be Josephine." Josie's feet almost left the ground as her uncle gave her a bear hug. She felt his moustache tickle her ear while her nose picked up an unusual, woodsy smell from his face.

Then holding Josie at arm's length, while his brown eyes danced over her, he said, "You look like your *Oma* Grün. That same small build, although you're skinnier. Same dimple on the left side when you smile." He hugged her again. "This is wonderful. My own family at last."

"Let me get your suitcases. You must be exhausted," he said.

"We don't have any luggage," Father said. "Just this paper bag from Vienna."

"Oh, of course."

Uncle Fritz led the way to a car. Just as Josie expected, it was big, new, had soft seats, and even a radio and a clock.

Father and Uncle Fritz sat in the front. With Mother beside her, Josie looked out the window. The streets were wide here: two trucks could drive side by side in the same direction. The buildings looked newer and brighter than the ones at home.

"Do we get a nice house?" Josie asked Uncle Fritz.

"I haven't found you a place yet. I want to let your parents look around first. For now you'll stay at my house."

They turned onto a street with large homes, each separated by stretches of grass and trees.

"There's so much space here," Father said. "How many families live in a place like that?"

"Just one."

"One? Then they must have big families to have such huge homes," Father said.

"No, some have one or two kids, some couples don't have any."

Father was as surprised as Josie. "Two people," he gasped. "Imagine."

Unlike East Germany, here the houses had many different shapes and were painted all kinds of colours, like pictures in stories Father read to her.

They turned into a driveway of a one-storey home. Josie had never seen this much grass between the street and the house. Even though it was past midnight, lights shone everywhere. Candle-shaped lanterns burned brightly at each side of the front door, although there was a street lamp nearby. Lights were on in most of the rooms. Would Father say anything? At home, if she ever forgot to turn something off, he told her not to waste electricity.

The door flew open before they even got there, revealing a smiling woman in a bright-blue robe that looked as if it was made of soft towels. The robe came down to her slippered feet and was held closed by a long belt tied into a bow at the stomach. Was it a coat? Or a long dress?

"Hello...Canada...welcome."

Josie knew those words, but the rest she didn't understand.

Uncle Fritz laughed. "My wife is so excited to meet you. But she doesn't speak German."

Everyone shook hands.

"This is Aunt Beth. This is Josephine. Come in; sit down."

The travellers decided to take a bath and have a late-night snack. Since they left Vienna, three days ago, they hadn't washed. After eating cheese and meat on crackers, Josie walked down the hall with Uncle Fritz. She stopped in the open door to the bathroom and stared. Instead of bare walls and a floor made of grey cement, like at home, this room was bright and colourful, with a toilet, a sink, space on a counter top, and both a tub and a shower. She had never seen all these things together in one room, not even in the hotel in Vienna.

Josie felt shy, but she wanted to ask questions too. "Why is the toilet in here?" she whispered.

Uncle Fritz smiled. "Because this is the bathroom. I guess you're not used to having everything in one room."

"But what if I'm taking a bath and someone else needs to use it?"

"We have another one, off our bedroom."

Two toilets for one family? Josie could hardly believe her ears. While Uncle Fritz ran water into the tub, he put something in it that made the whole room smell nice.

"Do you have clean underwear and pajamas?"

"No. I have to sleep in my summer dress. The Red Cross gave me one extra pair of panties and I wash them every night in the sink."

"Here, use Aunt Beth's spare housecoat." Her uncle gave her another long robe, pink this time. "A housecoat,"Josie mumbled to herself.

While she waited, Josie looked around. She had never seen a toilet seat with a lid. The toilet paper was soft, not rough like at home. The towels hung on straight rods. And the mirrors: there were so many of them. In East Germany they had one small mirror, as big as a plate, that hung by the kitchen sink. They had only had two showers, no tubs, to share with all the families on their floor in the apartment block. And of course the toilets, to be shared by everyone, were in a separate room down the hall.

Her uncle brought in a long, red nightgown with white flowers.

"This one is warm. You can keep it."

"Aunt Bez doesn't mind?"

"No, she said it's yours. But her name is Beth, not Bez."

"Bez," Josie said.

"No, no. You need to stick your tongue out between your teeth. Look. Beth, Beth."

"Bez."

Leaving a dish of thin, crunchy things called chips for her to eat, her uncle closed the door, so Josie undressed while chewing on her snack and sank down into the water. Bubbles sprang up all around her. At home she and Greta had blown soap bubbles outside, but they always burst. Scooping up handfuls, she spread them on her hair, face and shoulders.

*

"Can't we see it yet?" Josie looked at the houses and fields flashing by the car window as they left Calgary behind.

"No, not quite," Uncle Fritz said.

Father, Uncle Fritz and Josie were on the way to their new home. For the last few days the two men had looked at places while Josie slept, helped her aunt, watched TV and cared for Mother, who was still sick. Now they were going to clean their new home and get it ready. Slowing down, Uncle Fritz turned into a long driveway.

Josie stared. "Is that it?"

"Yes. Just for now," Uncle Fritz said.

"It's so small. And old."

A shack no bigger than her uncle's garage leaned on the earth like a tired, old cow barn. It had no big windows, no colourful paint, no flowers or grass. Rejected, it stood at the end of the rutted drive in a field of weeds that stretched as far as Josie could see. Josie got out and followed the adults, kicking at the wild grasses that came up to her knees.

"Why don't we get a new house?"

"Because we're refugees," Father said, his voice barely loud enough to be heard. "Uncle Fritz's friend will let us stay here for free until we can build ourselves a new life."

"But you promised a new house." As soon as she said it, Josie knew she shouldn't have. Father was already angry.

Now he stamped ahead, yelling, "No, I promised you a new life, a better life."

Uncle Fritz put his arm around her shoulder. "As soon as your father finds a job things will get better. It's hard for him to sit by and do nothing."

When Father shoved it, the door screeched in protest. A cloud of dust lifted from the floor, choking the stale air with tiny particles that sparkled in the sunlight.

"Okay, let's air it out." Her uncle tried to sound cheerful. "We'll clean it up, give the thirsty hinges a drink of oil and nail these floor planks down so the door opens all the way."

"Let's get going." Grabbing the tool kit, Father started hammering the floor boards, making cobwebs quiver on the beams.

"Josie, you attack the windows." Uncle Fritz gave her arm a friendly little squeeze. "I put rags and a bucket in the trunk of the car. See that creek? Get water from there. We'll fix this place up in no time. Then we'll all feel much better."

Uncle Fritz whistled while he swept and mopped up the worst of the dirt. Father finished the floor, repaired a broken window and hung up curtain rods. He pounded and measured as if he were in a terrible rush. Glad to escape the noisy shack, Josie went to the creek to get clean water.

The dirt on the windows was dry and caked. The spider webs were sticky. When one stuck on her hand, Josie watched a big, grey spider scurry off to safety under the sill.

"Now you're a refugee too," Josie thought. At least the spider didn't mind living here. They were not the only ones who had nothing.

They spent most of the morning nailing, scraping, scrubbing, sweeping and wiping. Then Uncle Fritz brought in an armful of material. They sorted and measured until they found three small pieces about the right size for curtains. They used a big sheet to partition off a corner of the room, so Josie had her own tiny bedroom. Finally they hung a colourful piece on one bare wall for decoration.

"It looks so much better," Uncle Fritz said. "Now, we'll get furniture from the second-hand store. And a wood stove that'll keep you nice and warm. And you can borrow dishes, pots and pans and blankets from us. You know, Karl, you're a lot better off than when I first came to Canada."

"Yes, I know, Fritz. Thanks. We couldn't have done all this without you," Father said. "It doesn't look too bad, does it?"

The shed had no electricity, no running water, no bathroom, not even a kitchen. How were they going to cook food, or wash, or see in the dark? But Josie didn't ask, wishing instead that they could stay longer with her aunt. Father had said they needed to get on with their own lives now, after spending a week with their relatives.

She and Aunt Beth couldn't understand each other very well, but her aunt had shown Josie so many things that she had never heard of before. There was: a small stove that heated food quickly; a kettle you plugged into the wall instead of heating it on a stove; a jack-in-the-box that toasted bread and popped it up when it was brown; a machine that dried clothes. Josie was amazed they didn't hang the laundry on the line when the sun was out. She also had a bicycle with different gears and no rust.

And then there was the magic bathtub. Aunt Beth showed her how to turn a knob that made water shoot out the "jets", little holes around the side of the tub. Once when she wanted to take a hot bath she added lots of the crystals Uncle Fritz had used that first night to make bubbles. She turned the jets on and closed her eyes, dreaming of underwater adventures.

When the soap dish fell to the floor, she opened her eyes and jumped up. Bubbles popped everywhere around her, over the edge of the tub and onto the floor. Josie stared as bubbles crept up the wall.

"*Halt, halt*," she yelled, jumping out of the tub, almost slipping. English maybe. What was the word? Oh yes. "Stop!" she cried. The bubbles invaded her clothes on the floor.

"Stop, stop."

Aunt Beth knocked on the door. Quickly Josie put the housecoat on and unlocked the door. Her aunt walked in, her eyes wide with surprise, and turned the jets off. She started laughing. Josie looked from the bubbles to her aunt, who was laughing so hard she had to lean against the doorpost.

"With the jets...no bubbles," she said, chuckling some more. Josie understood: the jets were mouths that blew bubbles faster than she and Greta ever could.

By the time her aunt had helped Josie dry the floor, most of the bubbles in the tub had popped and....

Uncle Fritz tapped her on the shoulder then pushed the shed door shut. "Are you listening? I called your name twice, but I guess you were dreaming."

"Yes, Uncle Fritz?"

"Let's go."

They returned to the city where, after lunch, they borrowed a truck to look for second-hand furniture.

"Keep all the bills. I'm paying you as soon as I get a job," Father said.

"Yes, yes, Karl." Uncle Fritz lifted a kitchen table above his head, then slid it onto the truck. "If we fix this broken leg it'll work just fine."

The chairs were old and dirty. Mother wouldn't like them; she wanted everything spotlessly clean, even when it was used. After dropping off the first load, they went home.

"We'll finish tomorrow," Uncle Fritz said, as he sank onto the couch.

"Thanks again," Father said. "I guess all this is just too much for me right now without your help."

"Oh, don't worry about it. I'm glad Beth and I took this week off. It's not every day that we get to welcome new relatives to our country."

"Do you really feel this is your country?" Mother asked, walking in from the bedroom.

"I'm a Canadian now. I've been here fifteen years."

Mother coughed, sighed and sat down. But Father jumped up. "Eva, enough of this! You've moped around all week as if your world has come to an end. You wanted to leave East Germany too."

"No Karl, I didn't. You did."

"But you weren't happy there either. You need to stop feeling sorry for yourself and help out. We've been given a chance at a better life here." He walked over to Mother and put his hand on her shoulder. "Come on, let's make the best of it. We're a team."

"I suppose you're right." Mother sighed, gave Father a little hug and walked back to the bedroom, coughing.

*

Josie swung the empty buckets back and forth as she walked to the creek. She was tired of carrying water, tired of cleaning the furniture, the walls and the stove. She sat down on the bank to rest.

Even though she no longer had the flu or a cold, Mother was unusually quiet. And Father was working so hard around the shed that he rarely took a break. Uncle Fritz had explained that her parents were acting differently because they felt unsure about their future, and were worried about their responsibilities. They had taken Josie away from her home.

"It'll all get better soon," her uncle assured her. "It takes time to adjust to new-found freedom and to make difficult choices, in such a different culture. It can be too much at first. It was hard for me, too, for a while. And I didn't have a daughter to worry about."

"But I try not to be any trouble."

Her uncle hugged her and said it wasn't her fault. Her parents just wanted to make sure they had done the right thing for her future. Plucking a weed from the bank Josie threw it in the creek and watched as it bobbed up and down before it was slowly carried away on the flow.

This morning they had moved into the shed. When they arrived, Mother looked as if she would cry, but then told Josie to get water and start scrubbing. If her mother only knew how much they'd already cleaned! The bad smell, dust and dirt were almost gone.

Father had finished putting a door on the new outhouse. Now he was chopping wood with Uncle Fritz's axe.

Feeling like a workhorse, Josie plodded back on the path she'd already worn through the weeds. At the shed she dumped the water in a metal container.

"Ready," she said.

Her father carried the tub inside, placing it on the stove in which a small fire burned.

"When this is warm we wash ourselves. You first."

When they finished washing in Josie's curtained-off space, they ate supper: potatoes, cabbage and a boiled egg each. Josie brought more water in for the dishes. They had tea and studied English until it was too dark for Father to read the words.

Josie crawled into her bed, a wooden board with Aunt Beth's camping foam placed on top.

*

In the morning Josie put her dress on. Aunt Beth had washed and ironed it and had given her white socks to wear with it. Unfortunately, she still had to wear the old coat and shoes the boys in Hungary had given her. The coat hung on her like a sack, was the colour of rotten leaves, had a button missing right on her stomach, and frayed sleeves. The mud-coloured shoes were scuffed and too heavy, with thick soles and heels. Josie hadn't noticed these things when the boys first gave them to her. Then she was just glad to be dry, warm, and protected. Now that she lived in Canada, where everything was clean and new, she no longer felt right in them.

Moving the curtain aside, Josie saw that Mother and Father were up. The mattress they had slept on leaned against the wall; the table and chairs stood in its place again. They ate their porridge in silence, her parents deep in thought.

A car horn honked. Almost knocking her chair over, Josie ran outside, to greet her uncle. They were going to a church, to sort through second-hand items for the house.

"Your father finished the outhouse." Uncle Fritz walked over to inspect it. Josie felt embarrassed. Even though he was a relative, she didn't want him to see the shaky wooden contraption, or the pieces of newspaper they used instead of toilet paper.

"He's quite a carpenter, isn't he?"

"It's wobbly, and the door won't stay shut."

"You won't need it for long anyway. I may have found your father a job."

"A job?"

"Yes. Come on, let's tell them." Uncle Fritz grabbed Josie's hand. They hurried into the shed.

"Good morning," Father said. "There's been a slight change of plans. Eva doesn't want to go into Calgary because she can't speak English."

"Everything will be so different," Mother said. "I'm afraid to go into big stores like the ones I saw on TV. All those people will be trying to sell me things."

"Well, I have some news." Uncle Fritz ignored their comments. "You may have a job, starting tomorrow."

"Really? Where?" Her father jumped up.

"At a restaurant. Washing dishes. It's not a great job, but it'll...."

"I'll take it! I'll take it!" Father said excitedly. Mother smiled as she put on the coat she borrowed from Aunt Beth.

"Let's go then," Uncle Fritz said. "First we'll get Beth; she's still at home. Then off to the church and on to the restaurant to see about your new job."

SIX

Father got the job! Skipping beside Aunt Beth, Josie's feet danced, even though Father said they couldn't afford to move into a better place right away. They went to the mall, a building so big and with so many stores, Josie could hardly count them all.

Uncle Fritz needed to lend her parents more money. After putting a card in the slot of a machine on the wall, he pressed some buttons, and a screen gave instructions before it produced twenty dollar bills. Maybe when Father started his job, he would get a card like that too.

"Uncle Fritz, can you lend us more money, so we can buy a new house?"

"Josephine!" Father grabbed her by the arm. "How rude of you. Your uncle has already done more than enough for us."

"But it just comes out of a machine."

Uncle Fritz laughed. "No, Josie, the machine only gives cash from my savings account. That's why I pressed my secret code first. If I don't put my own money into my account, I can't get any out."

"Oh." Josie didn't understand. She had never had her own money and didn't know what an account was. But there were so many things she didn't understand. For instance, why didn't people bring bags from home when they went shopping? In East Germany they always did. But Uncle Fritz said they didn't need any because the store attendants put the things in free, large paper or plastic bags for you. Imagine that: more bags every time they went shopping! Aunt Beth *bought* different sizes of plastic bags for sandwiches and other foods and the free ones she threw in the garbage. She also used paper towels to dry the counter, when she had a dishcloth in the sink.

When they walked into the grocery store, the doors opened by themselves. Josie looked for a doorman or a cable that pulled the handle, but she didn't see either.

The store was so big even Mother got excited. "Karl, look at all the food, so much of everything," she said.

"Bananas. I've seen pictures of them," Father smiled.

Everything looked and smelled fresh, clean and colourful. At home fruits and vegetables were never fresh in the store.

"Since you don't have a fridge, maybe you should buy some processed foods. You can heat them on the wood stove," Fritz said.

"Processed foods?" Mother asked.

"Yes, here, I'll show you." Leading them to a shelf, Uncle Fritz held up a box with a picture of pieces of yellow rope on it. "You just add water. Then you cook it, and it's ready. It's called macaroni and cheese."

Josie looked around for the store owner, or a guard. No one was there. "Can you just take things from the shelf?" At home the food was behind *Herr* Rosen, the baker's, or *Frau* Lehmann, the grocer's counter. They'd be accused of stealing if they touched anything.

"Sure. Just take what you need and put it in the cart. We pay over there." Uncle Fritz pointed.

They got one box, but Mother didn't want any more saying, "I can't read the directions. I want bread, potatoes and cabbage. I don't know how to make this."

"Mother, look at the chicken." Josie had never seen meat all cut up and wrapped in little packages. At home, at times when they could afford to buy meat, Mother had bought a live chicken and had killed and cleaned it herself.

There was hardly any line-up at the checkout— not like at home where they sometimes waited for more than an hour at each shop. After Father paid, they went to Uncle Fritz's house.

A woman at the church had allowed Aunt Beth to take several boxes of donated items home and now they sorted through them.

"Keep whatever you need. We'll put the rest back in the boxes and return them to the church for others," Uncle Fritz said.

"There are other poor people in Canada?" Mother's eyebrows shot up.

"Lots of families come to the church for help."

"But I thought," Mother looked from one adult to the next, "Canadians were rich."

"Some people have more than enough," Uncle Fritz explained, "but there are others, unemployed people and single parents, who don't have much. There are people who live on the streets and eat food from garbage cans."

Mother's face went pale. "Then why did we come here, Karl?" she whispered.

Uncle Fritz answered. "Because I encouraged Karl to come. Canada is a free country. You can say and believe whatever you want here. And if you work hard, you can have a good life. Karl can go from washing dishes to a better job. That's how I started. And look at me now; I own a garage."

Josie glanced around the room. Yes, Uncle Fritz had a good life. But then, why didn't the government make people share more equally? That's what her teachers said governments were for.

Aunt Beth held a red ski jacket up to Josie, who slid her arms into the sleeves and zipped it up. It fit as if it was made for her. She'd never owned a jacket, only makeover coats.

"I can wear this when I go skating."

"You like to skate?" Uncle Fritz asked.

Before she could answer, Father said, "We'll have to forget about skating for now *liebchen*, but it looks just right for school."

School! Josie's throat tightened, her stomach felt as if she had swallowed a pailful of icy water. Peeling the jacket off she threw it on the floor. She couldn't start school: she didn't know anybody. The thought of going to a place where they all talked like Aunt Beth, where no one could translate, petrified her.

The adults continued to sort through the boxes, holding up pants, dresses, hats, mittens, all sorts of things. From time to time Josie had to try something on, to see if it fit, but still wasn't happy when her pile of clothes grew higher.

Father said, "No shoes for you, Josie. Too bad, you'll have to wear the old ones to school."

"Uncle Fritz, can I stay with you and Aunt Beth for a while, to learn more English?"

"We'd like that, but we both have to go back to work."

"I start my job tomorrow and you start school on Tuesday," Father said. "The sooner we get on with things, the better it is for all of us."

*

"Das ist gut, sehr gut." Oma's voice rang clearly over the frozen pond. Frau Müller and Greta clapped as Josie skated backwards, then did a spin in the air.

"Ja, ja, she will be famous some day," Frau Müller said to Oma. "Look how she controls her body."

Josie skated harder and faster. The sunshine and the cold, crisp air made her feel she could do anything. She jumped and spun around in the air, once, twice, and landed cleanly. The blades of her skates carved sharp lines on the smooth surface of the pond.

She skated a half circle and again picked up speed for a jump. Suddenly she caught an edge and before she could catch her balance she fell to the ice.

Josie woke to the sounds of someone stumbling around in the half-dark room. In the candlelight grotesque shadows swept across the curtain.

"What time is it, Karl?" Mother's sleepy voice pulled Josie out of her dream.

"I don't know. I'll buy a clock or a watch today. Don't get up yet. I think it's still very early," Father said.

Josie remembered. This morning Father had to be at the bus stop by 6:25 so he could begin work by seven o'clock.

Her nose felt cold. The sheet swayed in the wind that blew through a crack in the windowsill; a howling storm lashed the creaking shed.

Grabbing the new jacket she'd been using as a pillow, Josie pulled it over her face. Today was her last day before starting school.

Long after Father had left, it began to get light outside. Mother got up and asked Josie to get water. In her pajamas and her old shoes Josie slipped out with the buckets. As she opened the door, the wind whipped it out of her hand and smacked it against the wall. A gust swept into the shack, blowing the big curtain right up to the ceiling, scattering some of the clothes from the table onto the floor and ripping a small curtain off a window.

While Josie dropped the buckets, Mother ran over and with her on the inside and Josie on the outside they grabbed the door and shut it. Turning, she saw the pails rolling, bouncing over the weeds as if playing game of tag. She ran after them and caught up with one when the handle hooked on a heavy stalk. The other bounded far across the field before Josie finally grabbed it.

She looked at the field that spread out to the horizon. Weeds bent this way and that in the fierce wind while clouds hurried along in the sky. Otherwise there was emptiness. In East Germany you could see this distance only from the top of the hill behind the town, if it wasn't a smoggy day. There you saw buildings, the river, other hills and the road.

After filling the buckets at the creek, she headed back, the full fury of the gale trying to blow her over. With most of the water spilled by the time she reached the shed, she put the buckets down to open the door. Both blew over, dumping the rest of their load on her shoes. She kicked the door in frustration, then clutched the handles before the wind could snatch the pails away again across the field.

For a second time she struggled to the creek and filled the buckets. This time when she reached the shed she wedged one half-filled pail between her shoes and added the water from the other one to it before opening the door.

"Only one? And you're soaked," Mother turned from the stove where she was stirring the porridge.

"It's the wind."

"I have to wash clothes today. I need at least eight more buckets full."

"But *Mutti*..." Josie set the full bucket down with a thud, spilling a few drops on the floor.

"Be careful. And don't argue. Do you think I like all this?" Mother turned back to the stove.

Without comment Josie spent what seemed like hours lugging water that sloshed on her and on the trail with every gust. After the first two trips she ate her porridge and changed into pants and her old coat.

The chairs hung with laundry made a ring around the blazing stove. Wet clothes steamed in a sauna.

"*Komm.* You must be tired." Mother's face dripped with perspiration.

"Mostly, I'm cold." Josie breathed on her fists.

Her mother wrapped her arms around her for the first time since they had arrived in this country. She smelled of soap.

"Things will get better, now that Father has a job."

"I don't want to go to school."

"Try it tomorrow. Maybe it won't be so bad."

In East Germany when a new boy had joined their class, others had teased and taunted him, especially when he cried about it. She wouldn't understand them even if they did tease her, but that didn't make her feel any better.

Josie watched while her mother repaired the rod for the window curtain.

"That spider again," Mother said, wiping the window clean of sticky threads. A grey spider rushed to the knothole in the ledge, but Mother tried to crush it.

"Mutti!" Josie jumped up and grabbed her mother's arm. The spider escaped. Josie sighed with relief.

"Why did you do that?" A wrinkle creased Mother's forehead. "Every day it weaves a mess on my clean windows."

"It's a refugee. We *have* to help it."

Mother shook her head and said, "I'm glad you're starting school tomorrow. You don't have much to do here."

For the rest of the morning Josie and her mother cleaned, studied English and made apple pancakes for lunch. In the afternoon they folded the dry clothes and sat by the stove, like they had done at *Oma*'s on cold Sundays.

"What was *Oma* like as a girl?"

"I don't know, *liebchen*. Remember, I didn't meet her until after I met your father."

"Tell me again how you met her."

"You like that story, don't you." They snuggled closer to the stove. "Well, the first time I was invited to *Oma*'s house your father was so nervous about me meeting his mother that he got the time mixed up. We arrived almost two hours early for afternoon tea and cookies. *Oma* was still dressed in her work clothes, not her visiting clothes, and her hair was in curlers. She had just started to get the bowl out to make cookies. I offered to make cookies while she changed.

"Your father showed me where things were kept and I got flour, butter, an egg yolk and powdered sugar. I measured and mixed and your father helped me cut them with the edge of a small glass.

"When *Oma* finished changing—I still remember she wore the green dress with beige stripes—we had tea and cookies. But when I bit into the first cookie, it was like cement. *Oma* couldn't eat one either.

"She asked what I had baked and I listed the ingredients of my favorite recipe, sandcookies.

"'Oh dear, oh no,' *Oma* said suddenly. She showed me where the powdered sugar was kept. What I had used, from the tin your father gave me, was cornstarch."

Josie laughed, even though she had heard the story many times. "So what did you do then?"

"*Oma* made jam sandwiches for us to eat while we painted half the cement cookies black and the other half white. *Oma* said she'd wanted a new checkers game anyway and was glad I'd helped her make one."

While her mother was peeling potatoes, Josie saw the spider leaving its hole. Grabbing a cup, she caught it on the glass and, holding her hand over the opening, went behind her curtain. She let the spider go and watched it disappear into a crack in a plank.

*

Nervously Josie clutched the plastic bag with her sandwich and an apple. Then she put it down and combed her hair again. If only they had a mirror. She touched her hair in the semi-darkness.

"Let's go," Father said.

They were catching a local bus into the city, where Father had promised Josie a big breakfast at the restaurant. After breakfast school would start.

Mother kissed her and wished her good luck in German.

"Only speak English from now on, Eva," Father said. "It's better."

Without replying, Mother turned to the stove.

Picking her lunch up again, Josie followed her father into the cold morning. Cars zoomed by on the road while he checked the time on his new watch.

When the bus came, they waved it down, climbed on board and headed for the city. After they got off the bus, they walked past a sporting goods store.

"*Vatti*," Josie started, but then decided against pointing at the skates she saw in the front window. They walked toward a building with a flashing sign. Through the large window Josie saw tables with red benches on either side.

"Come to the kitchen," Father said as they stepped into the restaurant. Josie still found it strange when her father spoke to her in English.

"Good morning," Father said, walking through the swinging door.

A man turned from a grill. "Good morning, Karl," he said. Then he turned to Josie, smiled and said, "Hi, I'm John."

"This is Josephine. Sit here," Father said, patting a stool.

Josie perched on the edge of the stool and watched John frying food on the grill.

"Hungry?" John asked.

"Yes," she whispered shyly.

"Bacon and eggs," John said, pointing. "For you."

Bacon and fried eggs for breakfast? How strange. That was food for the midday or evening meal. Josie had never eaten that in the morning.

"Hash browns, toast, jam," John explained while he put a plate of food in front of her. "Orange juice."

Josie laughed. What an unusual meal! But Father got one too and started eating.

"Father, I don't know the English for this, but why are we having dinner now? Fried potatoes and meat."

"Canadians don't just eat porridge or bread and tea in the morning."

John put Josie in charge of making toast, while he arranged orange slices on plates and made French toast and waffles. Father washed and sorted dishes, looked after the garbage and helped John when he got too busy. Sometimes they spoke in English while Josie listened, though she understood little.

Pointing to his watch, Father said something in English to Josie and held out her jacket. When they left, Josie's stomach lurched.

"I think you'll like this school; it's so much more relaxed than your old school," Father said.

School, that was *schule* Josie knew. Father spoke as fast as Canadian people. "*Ich weiss nicht,*" she shrugged.

So he repeated in German, "I guess you can't quite get all the words yet. But soon there won't be any more German, so study hard."

She *had* studied hard, for four weeks now. But people just talked too fast. When words were written down, Josie knew what some of them were because she had memorized them. But when people spoke the words were different, backwards and upside down.

The school wasn't far from the restaurant. As they walked up, a yellow bus pulled onto the grounds.

"You're going home on a bus like that," Father said. "They're just for school children."

"Where will it take me?"

"Home. You get off right at our driveway."

"Do I have go to a political youth group after school?"

"No, they don't have those here. People are free to do what they want after school or work."

Josie looked at the new, one-storey building. It was not at all like the old, grey stone school in East Germany. There would be no stairs to climb here. And where were the rows of bicycle racks? There was a playing field much larger than the one at home, but it had candy wrappers and other bits of garbage on it. If there was litter at her old school everyone had to stay for a lecture. Anyway, no one ever brought candy to school and everyone went home for lunch.

A few children ran out the front door, yelling and tossing a funny egg-shaped ball back and forth and running around on the field. And even though the bus unloaded a snake of children, the grounds still looked empty.

Another bus drove up. Josie noticed that most of the older students carried colourful bags, while the little ones had boxes. She hid her plastic grocery bag behind her back. Most girls wore pants to school, she saw, looking from them to her own East German dress, bare legs, sock and her old shoes. Everyone else had running shoes.

She followed her father, who walked right through the front door and up to the office. Last night he had told her that the principal was a woman, named Ms. Green, the English word for their own last name, Grün. He told her Josie would like her because she seemed friendly and chatty, rather than stern.

Gripping the top of her lunch bag in her left fist, Josie wiped the perspiration from her right hand. But, when the principal met them, she and Father didn't shake hands. They only stood, smiled and talked to each other.

Father introduced Josie. She held her hand ready for a shake, the way her parents had taught her. But when the principal didn't notice it, Josie took the edges of her dress and curtsied instead. Hearing laughter behind her, she turned to see two girls walking away, giggling. When they saw her, they curtsied too, said something to a boy who arrived, pointed and curtsied again. Josie's stomach churned.

Father touched her shoulder. "*Komm*, Ms. Green will introduce us to your teacher."

Boxes that stood on their ends, almost as big as coffins, lined the walls of the hallway. Two girls put their bags in one, then looked at themselves in a mirror on the inside of the door. Josie wished she could glance at her own hair, but was afraid to walk closer. She noticed the girls' earrings. Then, when one of them put lipstick on, Josie felt her mouth drop. Even Mother didn't wear make-up unless she went to a performance or an important meeting.

The principal talked to a short, curly-haired man, the teacher for grade six, Josie guessed. While he walked toward them, Josie again readied her hand for a shake.

Ms. Green spoke slowly, "Mr. Walters, this is Karl Grün. Mr. Walters is our grade six teacher." The teacher shook Father's hand. "This is Josie Grün." Josie had her hand ready, but Mr. Walters didn't notice it either.

He just smiled and said, "Hi, Josie, welcome." "Your teacher will put you on the right bus after school," Father said, in German. "Bye. Have a good day. Listen to your teacher." He left with Ms. Green.

Josie followed Mr. Walters to an empty desk and sat down.

SEVEN

After the teacher left, the girls who had put make-up on walked into the classroom. They studied Josie from her head to her toes, as if inspecting a piece of clothing at a market. Josie wished she could take her shoes off and hide them in her desk. She knew her face was turning red; she felt the heat creeping up from her neck. She must look so strange to them, with her old clothes and her wiry legs and arms that still showed the last marks from the measles. The girls both had short hair. Josie felt her own shoulder-length hair, cut by her mother at Aunt Beth's place last week, and wished again that they had at least had a mirror this morning. One girl, dressed in jeans and a blue T-shirt, nudged the other, who wore red pants and a flowered top. While talking in whispers, they giggled, turned and walked to the other end of the room.

A tall blond boy in a blue tracksuit walked in. "Hi," he said.

Josie swallowed and said, "Hi."

Sauntering over to her desk, he started talking.

But Josie couldn't understand him; she didn't catch a single word. Why did he talk so fast?

The boy waited, looking directly at her. Cringing, Josie tried to make herself smaller. She looked away. The boy said something again, only louder. And again, louder still.

"*Ich weiss nicht...*" Josie started. Then she stopped, wishing she could crawl inside the desk. It was no use. The boy didn't understand her any more than she did him. When Josie said nothing, he shrugged and walked out of the room.

Josie put her sandwich in the desk.

Three boys strolled into the classroom. One of the girls pointed to Josie and said something to them. Taking long steps, the biggest of the boys came over to her. He looked mean, with strong arms, fat legs in black pants, and very short hair.

"Hi," he said, while he held out his hand. Josie jumped up. He wasn't mean; he wanted to shake hands. She held hers out. "Hi."

"Bob." He grabbed her hand, squeezed it hard and shook her arm.

Bob said something she didn't understand. The other two boys and the girls moved closer, forming a ring around Josie.

Bob kicked one of Josie's shoes. Then he picked up the bottom of her dress and pulled it out as if to check the width of it. He whistled. The others laughed. Bob was saying things to the other children, but Josie understood none of it. At the same time he rotated Josie's shoulders to make her spin around. Then he motioned for her to turn on her own. She did, slowly, wiping her sweaty palms on her dress.

Why did they make her do this? Then she stood still, feeling dizzy and wanting to sit down.

Bob said something while he took the bottom of her dress again. In one quick move he lifted it up almost over her head. Everyone laughed loudly. The dress fell back down. Josie's knees wobbled. At home lots of boys tried to lift girls' skirts, but never too high. Besides, there she was with her friends. Or she could tell her teacher. Here she was helpless, alone.

The students quickly turned away from Josie when Mr. Walters walked in the door, his hands in his pockets. He said something. Some of the kids answered, laughing. Were they discussing her? How could the teacher talk to them like that? He was so friendly with them, not at all like at home.

The girl with the red pants motioned for Josie to follow her, but when Josie stayed at her desk, the girl came over, took her arm and said something. The teacher signalled for Josie to go along, so she went with the girl into the hall, where they walked past the narrow doors until the girl opened one and said something. She pointed to Josie. "Yours."

When the girl indicated Josie should hang her jacket on the hook, she did. Then they moved farther down the hall, until they came to a door that said "Girls." Josie knew that word.

She walked in. The stalls didn't go all the way up to the ceiling or down to the floor, so others could see her feet.

She went into one of the cubicles, just to be alone. Blowing her nose, she sat down for a while. It was quiet. The girls must have left. She heard a noise above her and looked up. Two faces peeked over the door. Josie jumped. Giggling, they disappeared.

As Josie left the washroom, a loud bell rang signalling the beginning of classes. The students didn't march in straight lines, and no teachers quieted them down.

Josie rushed into the classroom and sat at her desk.

*

Time passed very slowly that first morning. Josie understood the subject they started with, math, because the grade six questions on fractions were easy: at home she had done those in her third and fourth years. She didn't grasp the teacher's directions, but when she was the first to complete the whole page, with a borrowed pencil, Mr. Walters marked them all right. He patted her on the shoulder and seemed as pleased as Josie was. For once she didn't finish last.

If school was this easy, maybe she could do well in other subjects too, after she learned more English. But even with concentration it was impossible to pick out a few words from the flood of strange sounds.

Most of the morning she sat up like the teachers at home had taught her: feet flat on the floor, back straight, hands folded on her desk. The others leaned on their elbows or swung back in their chairs. Once a boy put his feet up on the desk during reading. At home, if anyone was ever brave enough to try that, the teacher would hit the student's legs, or at least make him stand beside his desk all morning. But Mr. Walters said nothing.

He was not very strict. The students talked a lot and yelled things out without even putting up their hands. Mr. Walters wrote on the shiny surface of the machine with a lighted square above it and magically the words showed up on a screen. At home the school had only one screen, in the gym.

Mr. Walters wrote down words the students called out, made circles around some and lines from one to the other. Finally the students stopped talking and opened their notebooks. Josie noticed that some of the children around her had scribbled all over the front of their books. At home only bad students wrote a word on the cover and the teacher always punished them.

Everyone started writing and it grew quiet, except for the scratching of pens. While Mr. Walters came up to her desk with paper, Josie noticed girls talking. Mr. Walters saw it too, but he did nothing about it. As he walked by, he even smiled at them. How could anyone learn this way? He sent no one out of the room; nobody stood in a corner. The students weren't even afraid of him.

Mr. Walters put a blank sheet of paper and felt-tip pens on her desk. Josie tried to smile, but then she looked away. Patting the felt-tip pens, the teacher wrote "My town in East Germany" at the top of the paper. Did she get to draw a picture with these pens? At home only the richer children had felt-tip pens, and then only one or two colours. On Josie's desk lay twelve different shades.

The teacher nodded at her and pointed to the words. Josie knew "My," "in" and "East Germany," but not the other word. What was she supposed to draw? The teacher didn't give her any examples to copy, or instructions on where to draw things, or what colour to use first. He just patted the paper, said something and smiled. Picking up the blue pen, Josie hesitantly started drawing the horizon.

She expected Mr. Walters to yell at her at any moment, but the teacher just nodded, said "good" and walked away.

Quickly Josie wiped her sweaty palms on her dress. He said "good" and she knew that word. She worked on, drawing a boat, a small island and a setting sun. Then she added some red and pink clouds and waves. At home the teachers had taught her how to draw and now she remembered all the lessons about lines, shades and colour combinations that would make a picture just like one she had done before in her old school.

A while after she finished, the boy next to her bent over her shoulder and said something in a loud voice. Immediately, students flooded around her. Josie felt as if she was drowning. Mr. Walters smiled as he walked over and said something, pointing to the clouds and the ocean before holding the picture up high. Everyone clapped. They liked it.

The bell sounded and everyone left their desk as quickly as they had come. All the others went out of the room, but Josie collected the felt-tip pens and placed them on Mr. Walters desk.

Students were eating in the hall and milling around before going outside. Josie slipped back into the room and took her apple. Was it lunch time? No. The clock only said 10:20. This was the longest morning ever. Taking a big bite from the apple, she put the rest back with her sandwich.

No one else was in the room, so she decided to go out too. The hallway was almost empty now. At the end of the hallway some students stood in line by a big white bowl in the wall. Bending over it, a girl let a stream of water come up to her face and drank. Josie looked on as the girl stood upright and wiped her mouth on her hand. Then the next one bent over. She wanted to try it, so she lined up and waited until it was her turn. Carefully she twisted the tap. Nothing happened. Bending lower, she turned harder. Water shot out and hit her full in the nose. Snorting, trying to blow the water from her nostrils, she pulled back, while she wiped her face with the handkerchief she always kept in the sleeve of her dress. A girl behind her laughed and said something. She turned the tap and showed Josie how high the water curved.

"See?" she said. She pushed her long, dark hair away from her face and bent down for a drink. While continuing to hold the tap, she motioned for Josie to drink also.

"Zank you," Josie said.

"Sure. What's your name?" the girl asked, her brown eyes curious, but friendly.

" I am Josie." There, she said a whole sentence to a stranger.

"I'm Trish. I have to..." was all Josie understood before Trish hurried out the door.

*

Time crept along toward lunch while the teacher and the students talked. Josie didn't know what about, although she liked the pictures of volcanoes they looked at. Then the teacher reached up and pulled a large map of the world down next to the screen. Josie's old classroom only had piles of battered textbooks, a large paper map, a blackboard and a meter stick. Here they had so much more!

Josie sat up with a start. While she daydreamed, Mr. Walters had walked up to her desk and now he said something, pointing to the map. Oh no, please! She couldn't go up to the front all by herself, with everyone, especially Bob and his friends, looking on. She shook her head slightly, although she knew it was wrong to refuse.

When the teacher gestured again, her stomach cramped. Jumping up, Josie fled from her desk, not to the map, but to the door. Rushing to the washroom, she threw up. She sat down and cried.

Why wouldn't they leave her alone? Why was she singled out for everyone to stare at? And now that she had disobeyed the teacher, he would punish her. What happened to bad children in Canada? If she only knew the way to the shed, she'd go home to *Mutti. She* would understand.

The bell rang. Where could she hide? Josie looked down the hall; at the far end kids streamed out of classrooms. This side was still empty, so she ran to where she'd put her jacket. She jerked open the door and stepped in. The space wasn't as big as it looked from the outside. She was small, but with the shelves she couldn't stand up in it. Sliding down on her seat, she hugged her knees tightly and slipped the door shut as voices sounded.

It was dark, cramped, stuffy, but safe. Then all around her doors slammed. For a split second Josie's mind replayed the swim across the river, the gun shots and the searching lights. After a while the noises stopped, and Josie sighed with relief. No one had found her.

She could not stay here much longer. Her body felt crammed, a folded slice of meat between two slices of bread. The air was stale. Her mouth felt like the inside of a garbage can.

Pushing the door open a little, she peeked out with one eye. All was clear on this side. Opening the door all the way, she eased her body out, first her feet, then her doubled limbs. Standing up, wobbling on prickly legs, she took her jacket off the hook. Getting her sandwich from her desk was impossible. Besides, she didn't want food.

The restaurant! Of course. Father would be mad when he heard that she had run out of the room without her teacher's permission, but an angry father was a hundred times better than that room full of strangers.

When her legs stopped protesting, Josie sneaked out of the front door, ran across the playground and down the street. Finding the restaurant was easy, but she hesitated at the back door of the kitchen. What if Father had gone somewhere for lunch? What if he got angry? She had to risk that. Pulling the door open a little, she slipped in. John turned from the grill.

"Hi," he said. "Your dad...." Josie didn't understand the rest. Just then Father walked in through another door, carrying two boxes on one shoulder. His eyebrows shot up.

"Why are you here?" At least he spoke German.

She rushed over to her father. "*Vati*, I had to leave. I can't go back. They all.."

Father put the boxes down and hugged her.

"They laugh at me and they talk about me, and they do mean things to me, and I don't understand anything." She buried her head in his chest.

Father patted her on the back. "Have some lunch. Then we'll go back and ask for English lessons."

The thought of returning to class made Josie's throat feel tight. She watched the men work and smelled the food. Then, after sitting on the stool for a while, she ate a little of the soup John gave her.

Father walked her back, hurrying with big steps because the restaurant was busy; he really didn't have time for this.

While Father talked to Ms. Green, the principal looked at Josie and shook her head. Did that mean she was not allowed back into the school? Josie felt a mixture of relief and worry.

"Ms. Green says she's sorry you had such a bad morning," Father explained. "She says she should have asked one of your classmates to show you around and keep you company during recess and lunch. She forgot to tell us you have English lessons every afternoon. It's called ESL. Ms. Green will take you there right now."

"Will you come, *Vati*?"

"I can't, *liebchen*. I have to work. Don't worry; it'll get easier." Father gave her a kiss.

As Josie watched her father walk out the door, she almost gave in to the temptation to run after him. But Ms. Green put her arm around Josie's shoulder and led her away in the opposite direction.

The halls were empty; the students had returned to their rooms. They turned a corner and walked into a large room. Josie stopped in surprise. Like in her old school library, shelves of books lined the walls. But instead of the shelves just holding a few books, they revealed row after row of colourful spines. There were hundreds, no probably thousands, of books. And everywhere the walls were covered with bright pictures.

Ms. Green smiled. "The library."

Josie nodded. "*Das sind....*"

"Books," Ms. Green said. Directing Josie to a low shelf, she pulled out a few large, hard-covered ones. They were for little kids, Josie thought, when she saw the pictures with big words written under them. Ms. Green pointed to a ball. "Ball," she said. She looked at Josie.

"Ball," Josie repeated. That was an easy word, almost the same as in German.

Ms. Green introduced a tall man with a beard as Mr. Johnson. Josie hoped she could remember all these strange names, so different from Jädicke and Jäger and Von Dach.

The librarian helped her sign the books out. Then Ms. Green took Josie past magazine racks to a door in the far corner.

As they walked into a small room, a petite woman with shiny dark hair and twinkling brown eyes looked up and smiled. Josie felt comfortable right away.

"This is Josie," Ms. Green said. "This is Mrs. Lang, and Rosita," she pointed to a small dark-haired girl, "and Li," she patted a boy on his shoulder. At the church Josie had seen some people who looked like Li. Maybe these children were refugees too.

Ms. Green talked to Mrs. Lang before she left. Josie noticed that Mrs. Lang was no taller than she was herself.

"Sit down, please." The teacher spoke slowly. "This is yours." When Mrs. Lang handed her a book, Josie realized she hadn't even tried to shake her hand. Maybe she was getting used to things just a little bit.

After the children repeated some English words from a list, Mrs. Lang brought out a game board and cards. If they knew the word to go with the picture on their card, they hopped their token one space along the board to a cup filled with notes. Li reached it first.

Choosing a note, he opened it and read, "the playground."

"Oh good, we will go out to the playground," said Mrs. Lang.

What was a playground? Josie got up with the rest and followed them into the hall.

"Your locker?" Mrs. Lang asked.

Josie looked around. Mrs. Lang tapped a door, tugged at her own coat sleeve, repeated "locker" and pointed to Josie.

"*Ach so.*" Josie walked down the hall, opened her door, took her red "locker" out and put it on. The others already had theirs, and they were waiting at the door.

Outside they walked around, repeating the names of objects on the field. Mrs. Lang made everyone take turns on the slide, then tried to balance herself and Rosita against Josie and Li on the teeter-totter.

Suddenly a flake of snow drifted down and landed on Rosita's hair. Another one followed, and another.

Mrs. Lang called "snow, snow." Josie felt excited but snow meant digging firewood out from under it, slipping on the path to the creek and wearing wet clothes in the cold air.

Then she noticed Li and Rosita's reactions. They stared at the white particles as if they were bugs. When Mrs. Lang asked them to catch some flakes and watch them melt, they looked almost afraid. At first Rosita pulled her hand back every time, as if she got an electric shock, but at last, after Mrs. Lang even ate a snowflake to prove that they were harmless, the little girl let one melt on her finger.

They went back to the library where they looked at a map. The teacher explained how it snowed in all the countries closer to the North and South Poles. Even though Josie didn't grasp most English words, she understood. The other two looked confused; they had probably never seen snow before.

When Mrs. Lang asked each one to indicate on the map where they came from, Josie found East Germany right away. Li pointed to Cambodia, but Rosita didn't know what to do, so Mrs. Lang took her finger and put it on Guatemala.

After returning to the classroom, Mrs. Lang took off her coat and said "coat." Then she held her hand out to Josie, saying "jacket" and expected something.

"Jacket?" she said slowly. What was a jacket?

"Your jacket," Mrs. Lang pronounced it carefully and pointed at Josie's sleeve.

Hadn't she just learned that this was a locker? Josie pointed to her jacket and said "locker?"

"No, no," laughed Mrs. Lang, slapping her own forehead. "Sorry, come." She took Josie to the hall.

"Locker," she said, pointing to the narrow door. "Jacket," she touched Josie's sleeve.

"*Ach so.*" Understanding, Josie handed her jacket to Mrs. Lang. They went over the names of winter clothing. Josie hoped she could remember some of them. Already she had forgotten the words she had learned earlier.

After Mrs. Lang gave everyone some work to do in their books, she sent Li and Rosita to their rooms and motioned for Josie to follow her. They went down the hall, stopping at Mr. Walters' classroom.

"No." Before she could stop herself, Josie had blurted it out. She wasn't going back in. She only wanted to go to Mrs. Lang's class. How could she tell the ESL teacher that?

Moving a step back from the door, she said, "No, please, I not," in her best English. But Mrs. Lang said "yes" and something else, then put her arm around Josie's shoulder, led her into the room and stayed at the front with her.

Immediately the class fell silent. Josie looked at the floor, wishing she'd sink through it. Mrs. Lang spoke to the students. Her tone was different than the one she used in her own room. She sounded angry. Josie glanced around the classroom. She noticed that now the students spoke only after they raised their hands. Mr. Walters smiled encouragingly at her. Finally, just as the bell rang, Mrs. Lang took Josie to her desk.

Carrying her lunchbag and the library books, Josie followed Mr. Walters out to the line of yellow buses. The parking lot was full of vehicles. At home everyone either walked, rode a bike or took a public bus. Nobody, not even the teachers, went to or from school by car.

Mr. Walters introduced Josie to her bus driver, Mrs. Adams, who pointed to the front seat. A few minutes later the bus drove off.

They drove a long way out of the city; houses or farms stood alone in the fields. Josie looked out the window while from time to time the bus stopped to let some children off. Even though it was a dark afternoon, with the snow still falling, Josie could see her shed clearly in the wheat field, now covered in white.

She stood up. "*Hier*, please."

"Bye," Mrs. Adams said.

"Bye." Protecting her books under her jacket, she ran down the driveway.

Mother was waiting in the doorway. She said Josie was very brave and looked at her new books. When Father came home, they talked about ESL and she filled him in on the events of the afternoon.

Suddenly the door burst open and in rushed Uncle Fritz. "Karl, Eva, *komm, schnell.* Quickly. East Germany. It's all over the news."

"What, what?" Father and Mother both yelled.

"The whole government of East Germany has resigned. They're gone!"

They rushed out to Uncle Fritz's car and drove to his house. There they watched the TV cameras zoom in on politicians ducking questions as they slipped into taxis. There were interviews with Germans who danced and sang in the streets. Josie watch eagerly. She wished she were there in the streets to share the excitement.

*

Two days later, on November 9, they again hurried to her uncle's house. This time reporters talked about East Germany and cameras zoomed in on bulldozers punching holes in the Berlin Wall. People laughed, cried, sang and shouted. One man attacked the wall with a sledge hammer.

"*Freiheit*, freedom," Father cried. "Finally."

"Now we can go home, at last," Mother sighed.

"Don't get your hopes up, Eva."

"Why not? We're free to go back there now."

"But we have no money for the trip."

"We can save it. Then we'll go back."

"I think we have to give Canada a try." Father sounded determined.

Josie looked at her parents. She hoped Mother would not give in this time. She wanted to go home, to *Oma* and Greta and even to her old school. Was *Oma* celebrating right now and thinking of them so far away?

Josie walked to the shelf where a framed photograph of Uncle Fritz' family, taken many years ago, stood to one side. *Oma* was in it too, but she was a young woman then and things were so different.

EIGHT

Josie stretched her arms above her head, but then quickly pulled them back under the bed covers. Her breath clouded in front of her face; her feet felt like clumps of ice.

Today was the first day of Christmas vacation, so she didn't have to get up. And even though the shed was either too cold with the stove out, or too hot with the fire blazing, she liked the time at home better than school. She had nothing to play with, but at least here nobody bothered her.

At school she had not made any friends. Because her English wasn't good enough, she didn't talk to anyone except Mrs. Lang, who somehow always understood her. Rosita was too young to play with, and she cried a lot. Like Josie, Li was shy and didn't say much. A few times classmates had tried to include her. Once Jake, the tall blond boy who had tried to talk to her on the first day, had chatted with her. But when Josie didn't understand most of what he said, he gave up, as did some of the girls. So Josie just sat through most of the morning, doing her math, exercises in her ESL book or drawing pictures. She liked the afternoon classes with Mrs. Lang, but dreaded the bus trips. A couple of older children on the bus teased her about the library books Mrs. Lang helped her choose. And sometimes, when she left the bus to go to the shed, they called "Moo-o-o-o." Mrs. Adams, the bus driver, got angry about it, but they did it anyway.

Josie heard Father get up to start the fire. It was light outside already. Now that Father worked a later shift at the restaurant, he stayed in bed longer. Last week Josie was the only one to leave in the dark. She hadn't seen Father at all because she was asleep by the time he came home from work.

"Eva," Father said, "get up and have breakfast with me." Josie heard him crumpling paper and breaking sticks to start a fire in the stove.

"There's not much here. Eat at the restaurant with your English-speaking friends." She yawned and Josie could hear her roll over in the bed and gather the blankets around herself. The kindling in the stove began to crackle. Father shut the stove door.

"I think today I'll apply for a course, to study for a chef's exam. I've saved enough money for it."

"What about saving for the trip home?" Mother's voice was muffled by the covers.

"If I become a chef, I make a lot more money. Then we can save," Father said. "Come on, Eva." Josie heard wrestling sounds, then Mother giggled and got up. The mattress sighed as it was set on its side against the wall.

"I just wish I wasn't stuck here all day." Josie could barely hear her mother's voice.

"Josie's with you now for the holidays, it won't be so bad. And if I can get a better job, we'll have money to move into the city."

Josie pulled her cold nose under the covers. She wished *Oma* were around, or Greta, or even the spider. Maybe the creature had left the shed. She wished she could leave too. Sitting up, Josie put her old pants and sweater on.

"*Guten Morgen*," Mother said.

"Good morning, Josie," said Father.

Should she answer in German or English? Picking up the buckets, she slid her feet into the new boots Father bought with his second pay cheque. "I'll get some snow for tea and dishes," she said in German.

"Speak English," Father said.

"Leave her alone, Karl."

Father switched to German. "She's gone to school for over a month now. Why is it still so hard for her to speak English?"

Grabbing her coat, she flung the door open and hurried out. The chilly air urged her along as she scooped up snow and ran back into the shed, the wire handles biting her hands. Inside she dumped the snow in a container on the stove. A whole pailful of it melted into just enough water to cover the bottom of the pot. Her fingers throbbed.

"Use your mittens, *liebchen*," Mother advised, holding Josie's hands in hers. The tingling stopped, and Josie went back out with her mittens, hat and scarf. She brought in ten buckets of snow before the pot was filled with water. The shed door stood ajar. Mother was cooking, and the windows didn't open.

"No sugar or milk today. We're out," Mother said when everyone sat down to breakfast. Silently they ate their oatmeal and drank their tea.

Josie wanted to talk about the decorated store windows she had seen from the bus, but she didn't know how to say it in English and dreaded speaking German with Father around.

A car pulled up outside the shed.

"Uncle Fritz!" Josie jumped up and ran outside.

"Hi Jos, how are you?"

"Fine."

"Your aunt wants to take you shopping today."

"*Guten morgen.* I see you're warm in here," Uncle Fritz said in German.

"We manage." Father cleaned the extra chair off.

Why was it okay for Uncle Fritz to speak German with Father even though he'd been here a lot longer than any of them?

Mother poured another cup of tea.

"I have a big surprise for you." Reaching into his pocket, her uncle took out a letter and handed it to Father. "From your mother."

From *Oma* Grün! Josie leaned closer. Mother pulled her chair in too. Father opened the letter and a small piece of paper dropped on the table. He unfolded it. Inside were a few tiny pieces of rock.

"Just read," Uncle Fritz said, when Father looked at him.

My dearest family,

Now that I am over the shock of your disappearance, and Hans has told me that you

92

*are safely in Canada, I can write to you. At first
I was angry that you didn't take me with you,
but I suppose your journey was too difficult for
me at my age. I miss you all terribly.*

*The police sold your belongings and rented
the apartment.*

"What they didn't steal for themselves first," Mother said. Josie thought about how she had left her skates on her winter dress. Who used them now?

*Much has changed here since you left. The
government resigned. Many of them now have
to answer for their actions. If you were here,
Karl, you could publish your articles without
any problems. You'll be happy to know that
your writer friend, Johann, was released from
jail. It's quite safe to send me letters. Did you
know the Berlin Wall is coming down? Here are
a few pieces of it, as a memento of the courage
you've shown. I got it from your cousin Wilhelm,
who went to West Berlin.*

Father cleared his throat. He fingered the fragments of rock.

*Write back soon, especially my Josie. Perhaps
when you are settled, I might join you in Canada.
We can leave more easily, now that the borders
are finally open again. I love you all and think
of you every day.*

Mutti

Father cleared his throat again and put the letter down. Even though Mother had a smile on her face, her eyes were filled with tears. Josie rubbed her hands in excitement: *Oma* might join them!

For a short while it was quiet. Everyone let the good news sink in before they started talking politics.

Josie reread *Oma*'s letter. Strange how they had been forced to risk their lives to flee from their own country because the borders were closed, while now, a few months later, East Germans could easily travel to West Germany if they wanted to. Josie had never seen the wall other than in pictures, and now in her hand were pieces of the concrete that had held searchlights, machine guns, guard towers and barbed wire.

Josie turned her attention back to the adults' conversation. Her uncle suggested that Mother might get a job as well, so they had enough money to move to an apartment in the city.

"You can't stay here all winter," he said. "It gets too cold, and we'll have more snow soon."

Josie hoped her parents would agree. Already it was hard for Father to get wood for the stove. The adults decided to go into the city together, first to look for a cheap apartment—Father said, "we'll just check,"—then to drop him off at work. Uncle Fritz would help Mother look for a job while Josie went shopping with Aunt Beth.

"I'll wash the dishes so we can leave," Josie said. She couldn't sit still any longer.

"Just leave them soaking in the tub."

Mother never left dishes unwashed.

✳

After searching for more than three hours, they found an apartment that wouldn't be too expensive if Mother got a job. The place was old and dirty, above a corner store on a noisy street. The living room was not much bigger than the shed, but it also had a kitchen with a stove and a fridge. Josie noticed her mother's eyes brightening when Uncle Fritz told them the landlord said they could rent it.

Josie would get the only bedroom. She would write Greta about it. Until today she hadn't been allowed to write her because Father worried that Greta's family might get into trouble if the police found out that they corresponded with escapees. But now, with the borders opened, she'd ask again.

Uncle Fritz paid a deposit. Mother took the keys, clutching them as if they were pure gold. Tomorrow they'd move.

They celebrated at the restaurant with tea and apple pie. Father explained that *à la mode* meant you got ice cream on your pie. Imagine two desserts at once!

Uncle Fritz dropped Josie off at his house before taking Mother on a job hunt.

Aunt Beth opened the door. "Come in." Walking into the living room, her aunt held up a dictionary. "English-German," it said. She searched through the pages and showed Josie "shop" in German.

"Yes, please." Josie knew that word anyway.

"Christmas, *Weihnacht*," Josie read next. She nodded.

"Presents." Trying the new language on her aunt wasn't nearly as scary as trying it at home. Aunt Beth clapped her hands and nodded.

"Yes, we'll shop for Christmas presents. Your English is very good." With the dictionary in her aunt's purse, they walked arm in arm out of the house, just like with *Oma*.

The mall was crowded with shoppers. Josie was fascinated by all the Christmas decorations: pictures of Santa Claus, trees with real lights, stars, balls, bells, cookie houses, wrapped boxes with ribbons....

Aunt Beth took Josie's hand. Leading her to a store full of chocolates, she chose several different kinds. Farther along, in a window, a paper sleigh with Santa and his reindeer flew back and forth on strings. Aunt Beth led Josie to a line of people and a big chair where Santa Claus sat by a camera. A woman in a green costume took pictures of him with the shoppers. Loud music played all around them.

"Picture Santa," her aunt said, pointing.

"Yes." Josie felt embarrassed. Why were adults so impressed with a man dressed up and taking pictures? Of course, getting presents *was* nice. In Canada that's what Christmas meant to many kids, she'd learned at school. It wasn't at all like that at home, where Father Christmas wasn't in every store. People gave small gifts in East Germany too, but mostly they celebrated peace, by visiting with family or friends, lighting candles, singing and listening to concerts. *Oma* would be lonely this year. Where would she go? Who could she visit?

The photographer took their picture, and they continued down the mall. Josie walked along beside her aunt, eyes wide in amazement. If Greta could see this!

But Josie knew that even if she explained the nervous excitement, the crowds and the noisy music in a hundred-page letter, her friend would never understand. Gasping, she pulled her arms closer when someone accidentally elbowed her in the ribs.

As they passed a shoe store Aunt Beth turned in. "For you," she said. "A Christmas present."

Spotting a bin of running shoes, Josie pointed to a white and blue pair. At home she had never had a choice: whatever the store had, or what relatives gave her, she accepted. She tried them on and, when they fit, her aunt paid for them.

They elbowed their way into a clothing store where her aunt bought them each a pair of jeans. Now she'd look more like everyone else, that is, if her parents would let her wear these to school.

Her aunt bought a TV for Uncle Fritz even though they already had one, more clothes for herself, and a telephone. They owned two phones already, one in the bedroom and one in the living room.

They walked by a sports store and Josie noticed a row of white skates on a rack. She saw Aunt Beth glance at her.

"What would you like for Christmas?" she asked.

She shrugged her shoulders. Her parents had taught her never to ask for presents and hadn't her aunt bought her two presents already: shoes and jeans?

After some searching for the right words in the dictionary, her aunt said she wanted to help Josie buy presents for her parents as well. They ended up with a reading lamp, a set of towels, an English cookbook with measuring cups and bowls and a wallet. Loaded with bags and boxes they struggled home.

*

Josie closed the bedroom door behind her. For the first time in her life she had her own room: her very own door and walls. She walked to the window, opened it and looked out at snowflakes drifting down on the street below. Traffic waited for the light to change. A bus screeched to a halt. She closed the window, although the sounds didn't bother her. It had been noisy in East Germany too.

Josie and Mother spent the next few days cleaning and rearranging the furniture. Uncle Fritz bought them a second-hand hide-a-bed. The couch opened up into a bed, so her parents could sleep on it. Josie still slept on a mattress on the floor, but her room looked cheerful, with cushions Aunt Beth lent her and colourful pictures, including one of Katarina Witt.

The holidays passed quickly. They spent all of Christmas Day at Aunt and Uncle's who ripped the paper as they opened their many presents and left a mess all over the living room floor. It seemed so wasteful. Josie and her parents saved all their paper, smoothing and folding each piece and carefully putting it aside.

When Josie opened her last present, from Uncle Fritz and Aunt Beth, her greatest wish came true! It was a large and fairly heavy box tied up with white ribbon. When Josie carefully lifted the lid she saw a brand new, shiny white pair of skates. She could hardly believe her eyes! Josie looked first at her parents and then at her aunt and uncle. Hugging the skates to her chest, she danced around the room.

Once the opening of presents was over with, they had a German *stollen* for lunch and turkey, sweet potatoes and fruit pudding. But they had no special German music or storytime while sitting around candles. Josie missed *Oma*.

A few days after Christmas Uncle Fritz took Josie to an indoor skating rink. She was surprised to learn that, even though she had not skated for many months, she had forgotten little. She zoomed round and round the slick surface and wanted to go to the arena every day. But Father refused because it cost money to skate at the indoor rink. There was no free outdoor rink near where they lived.

The holidays were almost over and school started again tomorrow. Josie put her new jeans on. She wished Mother would let her wear them to school. But when she had asked, Mother had said, "No, you have a nice dress to wear. Always look your best."

Sitting down on the floor, Josie took out her ESL book and started reviewing the English words she'd learned.

"I'm leaving," Father called. "Behave yourself; study hard."

Josie, jumped up, ran out and kissed him.

"What will you do when we're both at work?" Mother looked over her shoulder, then continued to mash the potatoes. Yesterday she had started her job as a chambermaid at a big hotel, leaving in the early afternoon and coming home late for supper.

"I'll watch TV and study English," Josie answered.

"A woman at the hotel has German books. Would you like to read one?"

"Maybe."

"You always liked sports better than reading. Talk to your Uncle about skating."

"He's so busy at the garage."

"Take the bus to Uncle Fritz's house tonight."

Mother had a funny smile on her face.

*

Uncle Fritz turned the TV off after the hockey game finished. Josie sat beside him on the couch.

"Do you like hockey?" her uncle asked.

"Yes, I like how they skate," Josie said. She felt comfortable here; they always spoke German.

Uncle Fritz got up and took an envelope off a shelf. "Here. Your mother and I talked about it when I took her to work yesterday."

Opening the envelope, Josie pulled out a piece of paper and a card. They both had English on them.

Uncle Fritz explained, "This is the address of an arena. It's a few blocks from your school. Your mother and I paid for your skating lessons there, twice a week after school and on Saturday mornings."

"Ahhhh!" she cried, throwing her arms around her uncle's neck. "*Danke! Danke!*" She couldn't think of anything else to say.

"This is the name and address of your coach, Monica. She teaches a group of girls about your age. Your father doesn't know yet. You'll have to tell him."

He would be so angry! He'd forbid it. He had explained that lessons were too expensive and would take too much time away from her studies. She'd just go once, to see, before telling him.

NINE

Josie stood in front of the building marked "Arena" and another long word she couldn't read. She had run here from school along the route Uncle Fritz had shown her and, even though the wind nipped at her, her hands were sweaty.

Trembling a little, Josie walked into the building. From farther down a long, dark hallway she heard men's voices. Was she late? Would Monica get angry?

She took a few steps down the hall, then stopped, turned and ran back to the entrance, afraid that she might not know the right question, that she would forget how to speak English. Walking down the hall again, feeling as if she were going through the dark woods on the night of their escape, she warded off fear by practicing in her head, "Where is Monica?"

When she reached a door that stood ajar, she stopped. She saw a man with a shiny bald head sitting in a chair. The door opened and another man said "Hi."

From among a clutter of skates, coats and other pieces of winter clothing he stared at her. Josie froze, forgetting her question.

"Hi, can I help you?" another man asked.

Josie swallowed. "*Wo ist*, where is Monica?"

"Monica?"

"Monica. Yes. Teacher," she sputtered.

"Oh, you mean Monica Smith, the figure skating coach? She's not here yet. She comes at 4:30."

Josie hurried back to the front entrance. A clock around the corner said 3:50. Several people came in and out of the door, sweeping in gusts of cold air. A young woman, not much taller than Josie, walked up from the back hallway. She wore a training suit with a heavy, purple sweater and carried a bag.

"Hi, are you Josie?"

"Yes."

"I'm Monica. They said you...."

"I do not understand. Speak slowly please," Josie said, the way Mrs. Lang had taught her.

Monica sat down beside Josie and asked her about school, her English and her skating in East Germany. Josie had difficulty understanding the questions, but after a while words began to fit into phrases.

Monica explained that the group already had five girls and two boys, and that the others had skated together for the last few years. She hoped Josie would fit into the routine.

Following Monica to the bleachers, Josie put her skates on and glided around the arena, keeping away from a group of small children who were in the middle of a lesson.

"Good," Monica said, turning. "Nice. Can you skate backwards?"

What was backwards? "I don't know."

"Like this."

With Josie following her coach, they spent fifteen minutes skating, turning and going over different words.

Monica beamed. "Great. You're athletic, and quite graceful on skates."

After the small kids finished their lessons, a group of girls and boys around Josie's age came onto the ice. Monica called them all together.

"This is Josie. She's from East Germany."

"Hi, Josie." Trish, the dark-haired girl who had helped her at the water fountain on her first day of school, smiled.

"She goes to my school," Trish said to Monica.

"Great. You can walk here together."

For an hour and a half she was only aware of the ice, the group and their practice.

"If you work hard, you'll easily pass the solo," Monica said to Josie. "It's in the spring."

"What is a solo? What is spring?"

"You skate by yourself, for judges. If you get good marks, you pass. Spring is the end of our season."

All by herself, like Katarina?

*

On Thursday Josie wondered if Trish would remember to wait for her. She hadn't seen her since the skating lesson on Tuesday. Dawdling in the hallway, she looked around. Rosita, her dark hair in two braids, walked up. She held hands with another little girl.

"Hi Josie," she said. "She is ESL too," she told her friend, as the two skipped down the hall. Josie headed out the front exit and wandered across the playing field. Trish was nowhere in sight.

In East Germany she had Greta to skate with and there Father didn't mind. She hadn't seen her father at all these last few days. He was always either at work or studying.

"Josie, wait up." Trish hurried across the playground, her skate bag slung over her shoulder. "Hi. From now on let's wait...."

"Speak slowly please. I do not understand." Josie blushed. Trish wanted to walk with her, and Josie had talked to her in English, like she did with Mrs. Lang.

"Sorry. Let's wait by that door and walk together on Tuesdays and Thursdays." Trish waved her arms as she spoke slowly.

"Yes."

"Don't you have a skate bag? It's hard to carry your skates like that when it gets cold."

"No."

"I have an old one. You want to use it?"

"Yes, thank you."

While they walked down the street, Trish said, "Bob is in your class, isn't he?"

"Yes."

"Too bad for you. Everybody is afraid of him."

Had she understood ? "You, eh, like Bob not?"

"No. Nobody likes him."

"*Ja*, he is." Josie felt less alone; Bob must have been mean to other students too.

When they reached the arena, Trish led the way to a room with tables and a snack bar.

"Want some hot chocolate? My treat."

What was treat? "I have no money," Josie said, hanging her skates on a chair.

"Hey, can't you read?" The man behind the snack bar pointed to a sign.

"No skates on tables or chairs," Josie read slowly.

Trish put the skates on the floor before she told the man behind the counter that Josie was from East Germany.

"Josie, this is Robert."

"Hi, welcome to Canada."

"Thank you."

Walking over with two cups of chocolate, Trish put one in front of Josie.

"I cannot pay." Josie felt her face go hot.

"My treat. Do you have homework? I always do mine here." Trish took a math book from her bag.

"I have English lessons." Josie's face felt hotter.

"You can practice. You must be smart if you speak German and English. You speak better than I speak French. And I've studied French since grade two."

They worked in silence until 4:25, then packed up and prepared to go on the ice.

Monica bustled in, carrying a bag. "Trish, you get started with the others while I talk to Josie."

Pulling a used tracksuit and two sweaters out of the bag, Monica said slowly, "You cannot skate in your dress. These are for you. Please take them home." She held the bag out to Josie. "Put them on." Monica pointed to a door.

Josie walked to the dressing room. She liked the sky-blue suit. Although the red sweater felt softer, she pulled the yellow one over her head because it had a pair of winged skates on the back. Now she'd really fly! And she did. Monica told her twice how well she skated and how glad she was that Josie had joined the group.

Josie had learned the three jump with *Frau* Müller so she was the only one who did it without falling.

At the end of the session Monica said, "Dry land on Saturday afternoon at four o'clock. Upstairs."

"I'll wait for you at the door," Trish said to Josie.

"What is dry land?"

"We practice jumps on the floor, not on the ice. Like gymnastics. It's fun."

They left the arena, Trish helping to carry Monica's bag for the first block. Then they said goodbye, and Josie continued to the bus stop.

*

It was the last Thursday afternoon in January. Josie sauntered from her ESL class to Mr. Walters' room, where she sat at her desk and opened one of her library books. The novels everyone else in the class read were still too difficult for her, although the books Mrs. Lang helped her find were for older kids now.

Finally the bell rang. Grabbing her homework, Josie put her chair on her desk. She wanted to meet Trish and go to the arena right away so they had time for a snack. So far Trish had paid for hot chocolate for both, but today Mother had given Josie money.

"Josie, I need to see you before you leave." Mr. Walters smiled.

Walking over to his desk, Josie felt her hands become damp and clammy. "Yes, Mr. Walters."

"This week your math wasn't quite as good as it

usually is. Do you need some help with it?"

"No, Mr. Walters." Her stomach tightened.

"I can explain it slowly, after school."

"*Ja*, tomorrow will I better."

"You may go then."

Josie hurried down the hall to the exit and took a quick drink at the water fountain. With skating three times a week and practicing jumps in her bedroom, like they did on dry land, there just wasn't time for all her homework. If Father found out he'd be furious. Thinking about it gave her a twinge of guilt.

On Saturday mornings Father left early, to work at a German restaurant and to practice for his chef's examination. Josie knew she had to tell him soon about her skating, but something made her afraid to do so. If only *Oma* was here....

"Hi Josie."

"Hi Trish." Josie pushed her thoughts about home from her mind. "Sorry you have waiting. Mr. Walters wanted me to talk."

They walked to the arena and headed straight for the cafeteria.

"I have money for hot chocolate for you," Josie sputtered. Then without ever intending to, and searching for the English words, she told Trish about her fear of telling her father about her skating, about how much she missed her grandmother, about her trouble with English and the homework and the math.

"And now wants Mr. Walters teach me, more math after school. But I have ESL homework," she said.

"I can help you. Don't worry, everybody hates homework."

Josie was happy. Trish was a friend, like Greta.

*

Snowflakes floated past the classroom window.

"Let's celebrate the last day of February," Mr. Walters said. "Who's for making snow sculptures?"

Most hands went up and several students cheered. Mr. Walters put everyone into groups of four. He insisted that each group have two boys and two girls. Josie was with Jake, Bob and Cherrie, a new student who had arrived two days earlier.

"Let's hear you talk funny," Bob said, pushing Josie.

"Leave her alone." Jake stepped between Josie and Bob, who turned away and walked out of the room. Josie sighed with relief. She didn't like to be in a group with Bob, but at least Jake was there too.

Outside Mr. Walters assigned each group an area on the playground. "Work together," he said. "This is a group art project."

"Let's roll some big balls first and then we can see what they look like," Jake said.

Josie and Cherrie agreed, but Bob asked, "So who says you take charge?" He made a snowball and threw it at some of the students in the next group.

"Bob, no snowballs." Mr. Walters walked over. "I need to see you working with the others."

"In my school we voted on who takes charge," Cherrie said.

"Okay, let's vote, but we have to work together," Jake said.

"Whoever wants to be the boss," Bob said, "put up your hand." Cherrie, Jake and Bob put their hands up.

All three voted for themselves, so that left the choice to Josie.

"Who do you vote for?" Cherrie asked.

"Jake," Josie said.

Bob kicked snow at the others. Mr Walters had stayed close to their group, Josie noticed.

Now he said, "Bob, let me have a chat with you." He took him down the field and when Bob came back he started rolling a ball, like the others. They decided to make a dragon by putting three balls beside each other and putting one on top for the head. After packing snow around it, Jake sent Cherrie in to get rulers.

"We'll carve the bottom away from here so the tail goes up," Jake said. He showed Josie what he meant and they started cutting the snow.

"Bob, you do the scales," Jake said.

"What scales? It isn't a fish," Bob said.

Mr. Walters walked to another group, so Bob thrust his ruler into the air like a sword. He jumped around, pretending to be fighting with someone else, and stepped on the dragon's tail, which broke off.

Before anyone could say anything Jake jumped up and grabbed Bob by his jacket. He gave the bigger boy a shove.

"You did that on purpose," he yelled.

Bob punched Jake and the two boys fell in the snow, with Bob on top. He raised his ruler and whacked Jake across the forehead.

Josie wanted to pull Bob off Jake, but she knew she wouldn't be strong enough. Bob raised his ruler again but Josie jumped up and grabbed the ruler in the air, catching Bob off guard. He teetered. Jake pushed him off as Bob let go.

Mr. Walters came running. "Get up," he said, his voice angry. The boys brushed some of the snow from their clothes. Mr. Walters wanted to know what had happened.

Josie thought Jake told the teacher exactly how everything had started, but Bob said he was busy making scales on the dragon when Jake pushed him so that he fell and accidentally broke the tail.

"Josie, what did you see?" Mr. Walters asked.

"I saw Bob with the ruler, like..." she jumped around,the way Bob had done, "tail broke."

Cherrie told Mr. Walters the same thing. The teacher took Bob into the building. Mr. Walters came out again, but Bob didn't return for the rest of the morning.

"Good thing you got the ruler away from him," Jake said to Josie. "Thanks."

They rolled a new ball and carved the dragon, although they hadn't finished by the time the lunch bell rang.

"Let's eat and then we'll finish it," Jake said.
After lunch they went back out, but they weren't allowed to take their rulers with them this time.

Trish came walking up. "What are you making?"

"A dragon."

"Wanna help?" Jake said.

"Sure." Trish knelt down beside them and started making ridges of snow on the body, like the others were doing.

"I'm cold; I'm going in," Cherrie said.

"You still play hockey?" Trish asked Jake. "I never see you at the arena anymore."

"We play at six in the morning now." He made a face. "Too early."

"He used to play right after figure skating," Trish said. "Josie skates too. She's good."

"Really?" Jake smiled. "Better than you?"

Josie felt the colour creeping up her cheeks with pride. She looked and saw Li standing nearby, staring at the dragon.

"A dragon," said Trish, seeing Li too. "Like we did in class." Li nodded. Then he walked away.

"He's in my class. He's so shy," Trish said.

"He go to ESL too," Josie said.

TEN

At the arena that afternoon Monica had some bad news.

"I fell and I have a sore knee. It's nothing serious, don't worry. But I'm not going to skate much today."

Everyone stretched and bent on the walkway to limber up their muscles before going onto the ice.

"Swing your arms. Don't forget to move every part of your body," Monica yelled from one corner. She wanted them to practice their "shoot the duck."

"You're leaning back too much," Monica said. "Josie, show them how you do it."

Josie pushed off, went into a sitting position and stuck her left leg out in front of her. She brought her hands forward to hold her free leg while she glided.

"Look how straight her back is," Monica said. "And see, even her toe is pointed forward. Now everyone try," Monica said. "Josie, go around and let them know if they sit back too far, or if their leg isn't straight."

I'm a coach *too*, Josie thought.

"Like this?" Trish said as she fell on the ice.

"Your head so," Josie said, looking straight ahead. "Not look down."

"Oh yes, I forgot." Trish glided in a sitting position.

Monica wanted everyone to skate backwards for a while before she asked them to find a patch of ice and work on the three jump. She came around slowly, from patch to patch.

"Josie, you practice the loop jump," Monica said.

Frau Müller had taught Josie the three jump and not the loop jump.

"Remember to land on the same foot you jump with. Your other leg swings around." Monica used her arms and legs to explain things, so Josie understood most of the instructions. The coach demonstrated the jump, grimaced while she landed and said, "You work on it."

Josie jumped. She remembered to land with her right knee bent like a spring so she could have a smooth glide. Her left leg had to swing in a full circle. That threw her off and she usually landed with her body pitching forward. Then she had to put her hands on the ice to make sure she didn't fall. She knew she needed to do a better job if she wanted to do well on her solo. Monica had explained that the loop jump was the part the judges looked at most for this year's solo for her age group. If she wanted high marks she had to do it smoothly, with balance and control.

*

It was late March. The snow melted and spring sunshine stroked Josie's cheeks as she walked to the arena with Trish on Thursday afternoon. They had an agreement that Josie paid for a snack on Tuesdays, and Trish on Thursdays.

Although Josie only went to ESL for one hour a day now, because of her progress, she and Trish always did the ESL homework together at the arena. At four-thirty they put on their skates, sweaters and gloves and moved out onto the ice. A couple of the girls wore tights, leotards and legwarmers.

"I want to work with each of you to get you ready for next week's solo," Monica said. "While I do that, the rest of you practice your routine."

Josie warmed up, raced around for a few laps, then found a patch of ice to work on. If she did the loop jump properly, her solo was impressive, Monica had told her.

"Josie, let me see your loop jump."

Taking a few strokes towards her coach, Josie started on her right foot, rotated and fell.

"You still move your shoulders too quickly, before you are ready," Monica said, demonstrating what she meant. "It's getting better though. Concentrate on your shoulders because that's where you throw yourself off balance. Keep still, lean into the center and rotate higher into the air."

Josie tried again. She stroked, balanced on one foot, and started the jump, but her shoulders still moved forward too much, and she fell.

"Work on it for a while. Keep those shoulders back," she said, skating off to another girl.

After the work-out they left the ice, wiping the snow off their blades and putting skate guards on.

"One more practice on Saturday girls, and then there's the dry land upstairs," Monica said. "We'll work on some jumps, watch a video, and you'll be ready for the big day. Most of you will do well."

Monica sat down beside Josie. "Do you have a skating dress?"

"No."

"I thought you might not have one. Does your mother sew?"

"Sew?"

"Yes, on a machine." Monica made sewing motions.

"*Ach so, nähen.*" Josie understood. "Yes she can, but she does not have a sew."

"She doesn't have a sewing machine?"

"No."

"You can both come to my house on Sunday and we can make you a dress."

"I ask." Monica thought of everything.

As she left the arena with Trish, a horn honked.

"Josephine, *komm.*"

"*Ja,* my mother is here. I have to go." she said, running to the driver's side and hugging her aunt. Then she switched to German, as she always did when she saw her mother. "*Mutti,* whose car is this?

"It's ours. Uncle Fritz gave it to us. It's old, but he says it runs. Your father will use it to go to work."

Josie crawled into the back seat.

"Your father passed his chef's exam," Mother said. "On Sunday he's starting a new job as head cook at the German restaurant. He'll make almost three times as much money there. Things will be easier. I finished work early today, so let's celebrate with ice cream."

Just then Monica walked out of the arena, so Josie told her mother about the dress. They all got out to talk to the coach. Monica promised to give Josie one of her old dresses. She would drive Josie over to her aunt's place after dry land on Saturday and Mother would alter the dress on her aunt's sewing machine.

✳

On Saturday, Father had a day off. This was Josie's final ice time before the solo, so she couldn't miss it. Absent-mindedly she dropped some bread on her lap.

"Josie, pay attention to your food."

Already her father didn't look pleased, and she hadn't even told him yet about her skating.

"We are going to a friend's place in the mountains," he continued in English. "To help him..." Josie tuned the rest out. She knew Father had a day off, but she didn't realize he had made plans for them.

"When leaving we, *Vati*?"

"In half an hour."

What now? She wanted to skate more than anything. At the arena she had friends, she understood them, she wasn't afraid to speak English with them.

"I cannot," she switched to German: English just wouldn't come out right at home. "I can't go in half an hour. I have to go skating."

Putting his knife and fork down, Father said, in English, "What do you mean?"

"I," Josie tried English again, but went back to German. "I joined figure skating. Uncle Fritz paid." She almost whispered now. "I have a solo."

"Who gave you permission to join figure skating?" He must be angry: he spoke German!

"I did, Karl."

Josie sighed with relief. Let her parents talk to

each other about it. After all, Mother helped Uncle Fritz plan the whole thing.

"Without talking to me? Behind my back? What's happening to this family?" Father jumped up and started walking across the room.

"Karl, we have to talk about this."

"We certainly do. I work all day and half the night, to study for a better job, to bring more money home, to make things better for all of us. Today is my first day off in four months, so I plan a nice outing, with a hike in the mountains, and I find that my family made other plans, behind my back, without including me."

Putting his elbows on the table, he buried his head in his hands, mumbling, "I'm so tired of English, of studying, of washing dishes, of following other people's orders like a dog. I tried to make a good life for us. I guess I failed."

Josie jumped up and ran into the bedroom.

Mother followed her. "Josie, you'd better go to your skating practice on the bus. Your father is overworked. He's been pushing himself too hard. While you skate, we'll talk. Things will be better when you get back."

"What if *Vati* doesn't want me to skate?"

"We'll talk about that too when you come home. You'll skate your solo and after that we'll see."

Mother kissed Josie and steered her to the door. Fleeing from the apartment, Josie ran down the street, the skate bag striking her leg with each step.

*

Father and Mother were waiting in the car when Josie left the arena. As soon as she hopped in, they drove off. Josie noticed immediately that Father looked better than when she left the apartment.

Leaving the city behind, they watched fields and farms flash by, while the Rocky Mountains beckoned them westward. Her parents talked about directions, the traffic and the car, all in German.

Suddenly her father turned to Josie and said, "We're not going to my friend's cabin, we're going for a drive instead. It's time we relaxed as a family and saw some of the countryside."

Although Josie wondered what her parents had decided about her skating, she was afraid to mention it for fear of upsetting them. Quietly she sat in the back seat. Before long they stopped at a small restaurant for lunch. Josie had a hot dog and fries, while her parents had hamburgers. Josie was getting used to the taste of Canadian food now, but she could tell that neither of her parents really liked theirs. Her mother ate only half her hamburger.

They drove closer to the mountains and got out at a small stream. Mother spread a blanket on the sand, while Father took his socks off.

"Ah, too cold still," he said, quickly pulling his feet out of the stream. Everyone sat down on the blanket.

"Your mother and I want you to help us decide something," Father said.

Mother reached out and took Father's hand. "Your father would like to stay here. I often think about going back to Germany, now that the borders are open and East and West Germany will be one free country again. We want to stay together, but we can't agree on where to live. What would you like?"

"Me?" She paused and weighed what she liked better about her new home: Trish was her best friend, school was easier now, Mr. Walters was friendly and easy going and she loved Uncle Fritz and Aunt Beth. Finally she asked, "Can I keep on skating?"

"Does it really mean that much to you?" Father asked.

"Yes, when I'm skating I like Canada, I can speak English, everything is better."

"But do you have enough time for your studies?"

"Karl, she needs more than just school. She learns a lot at the arena. Her friends are there," Mother said.

"I guess in that case you can keep going, this year anyway," Father said, smiling at her.

"Then I want to stay," she said, looking from one to the other.

"Then we'll all stay," Mother said.

"Are you sure, Eva?"

"Yes. You both want it."

"Do you think *Oma* will move here?" Josie asked.

"We'll start saving for her flight," Father said.

On their way back from the outing Father dropped Josie off at the arena for her dry land session. She was late: the others were in the middle of practicing their jumps and stretches.

"Josie, I'm glad you're here. Warm up," Monica said.

Trish landed on the floor after a high twirl in the air. "Where were you?" she asked.

"I will tell you later," Josie said, while she stretched. Then she practiced her loop jump.

"You must have worked on that a lot," Monica said approvingly. "It looks great. I see you're keeping your shoulders back and you're getting high up off the floor.

It was time to watch a video: Katarina Witt at the Calgary Olympics with Elizabeth Manley, the Canadian silver medal winner.

"Keep a picture in your mind of yourself moving perfectly. Be positive," Monica said.

"That's us," Trish whispered. "You're Katarina Witt, from East Germany, and I am Elizabeth Manley."

After dry land Monica drove Josie to her aunt's house. When they got there, the coach met Father and Uncle Fritz, who were watching television. Mother, Aunt Beth, Monica and Josie went downstairs to the sewing machine.

"I thought this might look good on you." Monica pulled a shiny purple outfit from a bag. "I wore this in an ice carnival one year."

Both Josie and her mother gasped. They touched the soft material and pink flowers around the edge of the miniskirt that matched the band of flowers swirling down the front.

"See how it fits," Aunt Beth said.

It was too big, so Mother pinned it in on the sides and sewed it on the machine.

"You do that so easily," Monica said. "Maybe you can help some of the parents who have trouble."

Mother beamed, "Yes, I can."

"I also brought white tights, a white sweater and legwarmers for when you're waiting on the bench." Monica, like a magician, pulled the clothing out of the bag.

In her outfit, Josie looked at herself in the mirror.

"Wait untill you see Josie do her solo," Monica said.

"I'm coming to watch too," Aunt Beth smiled. "I can't wait to see her."

*

On Tuesday Aunt Beth and Mother picked Josie and Trish up after school and drove them to the arena. Since Ms. Green had wished all the school's skaters good luck on the PA system, everyone knew about the event. Jake came to the arena and he brought several of their classmates.

A group of small children were lined up to skate the Dutch Waltz. After changing into her outfit and leg warmers, Josie huddled with the other skaters on the bench under the heater. She shivered, more with excitement then from the cold. Moving closer to Trish, she pulled the blanket tighter around her legs.

After twenty minutes a voice on the loudspeaker cracked, "Warm up for the free style, please."

"This is it girls," Monica said. "Give it your best."

Josie's legs stiffened. Moving onto the ice, she took some strokes to get her body going.

"Good luck," her classmates called.

Josie practiced until the speaker announced the skaters' names in order.

"Line up for the solos: Bobbie Callum, Josephine Grün, Trish McKenzie...."

Josie was second in line. After taking her sweater, leg warmers and gloves off, she waited at the gate, her heart racing, her legs numb. In just a few minutes she had to skate alone while the judges watched every move she made. Suddenly she was sure she couldn't do it. She wasn't ready!

"Josephine Grün," the voice on the loudspeaker said. Josie skated slowly to center ice. She stood still and tried to relax as she waited for her music to begin, thinking only of the program that she had practiced for so long.

As the music came over the loudspeaker, Josie started her routine. She stroked to pick up speed, turned to skate backwards, turned again and crouched to a perfect "shoot the duck." A picture of *Oma* applauding flashed through her mind. Now her confidence soared and she thought of Katarina. She stroked again and took off for her loop jump, high in the air, her shoulders back, her free leg making a wide circle. She landed in a smooth glide. She stroked to pick up speed and completed a second loop jump. Again her landing was right on.

The rest of her program went smoothly and when the music stopped she curtsied in front of the judging area. As she skated towards the exit, joy bubbled up inside her; she could do nothing to stop it. Everyone applauded. She stepped off the ice and right into a bouquet of flowers and her father's arms.

"*Vati*!"

"*Wunderbar*," Father said. "You were great! You deserve to skate as much as you do."

"I didn't know you were coming."

"We weren't busy, so I decided to ask for an hour off work. And I'm glad I did."

While Josie's classmates whistled and clapped, Monica hugged her. Mother beamed. Then all quieted down for Trish's turn. With her heart still racing and her arms full of flowers, Josie watched as Trish skated around the ice. She made no mistakes. A few other skaters stumbled, two fell when they tried their loop jumps.

At the end Monica handed the judges' scores to everyone. Josie's sheets showed seven out of ten from two judges, eight from the third judge.

"Twenty-two! A great score," Monica said.

"Did I pass?" Josie asked.

"You sure did, with flying colours."

Josie turned to Trish."What did you get?"

"Twenty," her friend said putting her arm around Josie's shoulder.

"Come on Trish, join us," said Aunt Beth as they all walked out of the arena.

Father squeezed Josie's shoulder, "Who wants to celebrate?"

A big THANK YOU goes to

my Highland Park Elementary School 1990/91 class of Tamara, Serina, Brent, Kristi, Jarrod, Jennifer, Kristy Lee, Daryl, Brody, Mike, Adam, March, Perry, Faye, Brett, Bern, Andy, Shelli, Angus, Andrew, Erin, Jonathon, Jake and especially Amy Cohen for their enthusiasm and help when we worked on the manuscript as a class.

Also to my year 3/4 class of 1991/92 for listening so well, to the Kalamalka Writers' Collective for their never-ending encouragement, to Lorna Berndsen for teaching me about skating and to Ann Featherstone, Orca's children's book editor, for all her suggestions.

Ann Alma spent her first 23 years in Holland where she worked as a teacher before emigrating to Canada in 1970. She has more than two decades experience teaching in the Canadian school system and as an instructor of English as a Second Language, both abroad and in Canada.

She is the author of *Under Emily's Sky* (Beach Holme, 1997) and *Something to Tell* (Riverwood, 1998) and has published numerous travel articles in magazines in Canada, the United States and Japan. Alma is a co-founder of Kalamalka Press and has taught creative writing at Selkirk College.

She lives on a hobby farm in the West Kootenay mountains near Nelson, British Columbia.